I0543706

JUSTICE TURNS UGLY

BOOK TWO OF A JULIA LILLUS SERIES

JAMES ROBERTS

Edited by

JAMES ROBERTS

Illustrated by

JAMES ROBERTS

Copyright © 2019 by James Roberts Publishing

All rights reserved.

Cover Design Copyright © 2019 James Roberts

Cover Art Copyright © 2019 James Roberts

Cover Background by Dreamstime.com

Illustrations Copyright © 2019 James Roberts

ISBN: 978-1-7361234-2-3

Library of Congress Control Number: 2020923081

Published by James Roberts Publishing

Printed in the United States Of America

No part of this book may be reproduced in any form or by any electronic or mechanical means, including information storage and retrieval systems, without written permission from the author, except for the use of brief quotations in a book review. All rights reserved.

This is a work of fiction. Names, characters, businesses, places, events and incidents are either the products of the author's imagination or used in a fictitious manner. Any resemblance to actual persons, living or dead, or actual events is purely coincidental.

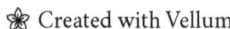 Created with Vellum

For those who have become victims of sexual assault.

And finally, to law enforcement and the court systems to bring justice where needed.

CONTENTS

INTRODUCTION

———

"Justice Turns Ugly" is the Second Book of A Julia Lillus Series and is a culmination of experiences intertwined with romantic relationships, erotic sex, mystery, and murder.

Each chapter of this book depicts character personalities, good and bad, underlining conflicts, and their resolution. I have opened the dark secrets of incest and rape, exploring the pain and devastation it causes.

A part of this book explores the most sensuous and intimate closeness human beings can experience through the erotic acts of the total consumption of each other which exhibits the true meaning of devotion in a relationship.

Throughout this book, the reader will experience anger, disappointment, vulnerability, and joy. The reader will discover the resolution to each of these emotions and finish the book with a feeling of satisfaction with hope in the future.

And finally, this book continues where Book One leaves off; to finalize loose ends and to introduce new adventures while introducing new characters.

PREFACE

James Roberts

Richard and Bobbie are enjoying their newlywed life which is just starting, while Julia Lillus thinks back on her relationship with her late husband, Timothy Lillus.

Bobbie and Julia are both confronted by the two stalking men who frequent the gym with undesirable results.

Murder and incest rears its ugly head in Harford and sends the Police Department into a tale-spin.

Babies are being born to young mothers as Julia finds new roles in her life.

In the end, the city of Harford has become quiet, once again.

LOVE AND REFLECTION

t the wedding, a conversation begins.

"Hello, Julia."

"Hello, Bobbie. I am so happy for Richard and you. You two make a great pair."

"Yeah, it took some time to get Richard's attention, and finally for him to realize how much I love and adore him. I thank you, Julia, for steering him away from you."

"What? Come on Bobbie, I did no such thing! I said nothing to Richard. He just finally realized there are more fish in the sea than just me. Besides, I am an old widow. He has a young Philly with you, Bobbie."

"You crack me up, Julia. You are beautiful no matter what your age or what you say. By the way, I haven't had much time to talk to you since being busy with all the preparations for the wedding. How are you doing? Are you OK? The Tim thing shook us all up, and I am worried about you, Julia. You had a massive amount of love for Tim."

"I am surviving, Bobbie, but I would be lying if I said the whole incident with Tim and I has stopped bothering me. Bobbie, I had been married to Tim for eight years. We had a very satisfying relationship. I still have trouble understanding what went wrong in Tim's head. The doctor told us Tim's issue was due to a recessive gene; it would be a crap shoot whether it showed up in his life. We thought, well I thought, he would get over it, and Tim was convinced he could control it. I feel the thing that didn't help in the matter, was our increasing romantic interludes."

"What do you mean, Julia?"

"Well, the activity in our relationship, which we both loved and pushed for, ended up ruining Tim...and us."

"I still do not follow you, Julia."

"Tim and I had a very erotic and active sex life. In the beginning, it was difficult, but the longer we were together, and the more we learned about each other, I found my panties off of me more than they were on; our sexual activities endured greatly. I feel because of those activities, Tim was enjoying me so much sexually, it stirred up his condition by realizing other men could also enjoy what I had to offer sexually. Of course, Tim got it all wrong, and it spiraled to where I am today."

"Julia, I am beginning to understand the trauma you are experiencing. I am sorry."

"Oh, don't be sorry, just love Richard and enjoy each other. I am so happy for you and Richard. I will see you back in the office in a couple of weeks?" asks Julia.

"Oh, yes."

"Don't forget, we have a date at the gym when you get back. We have carbs to burn."

"I won't, Julia."

BOBBIE AND RICHARD CONJUGATE

Bobbie and Richard travel to Alexandria Bay for their honeymoon stay. Both want a quiet and secluded place where they can relax and explore each other more thoroughly. The bay is an excellent place for them because the tourist season has just ended and there is no one around the hotel.

"Oh, Richard, it was such a great wedding reception, wasn't it?" asks Bobbie.

"It sure was, but I have to admit I couldn't wait for it to end so that I could get to know you more…intimately?"

"Oh, Richard, what do you have in mind?"

"Well…..," says Richard.

"I know, it has been quite excruciating for me, too. I am glad we waited for this moment of…intimacy? You are talking about 'that' intimacy aren't you Richard?"

"Sweetheart, I can see it is going to take me some time to get to know you," states Richard.

"Do you think so, honey? Let's see how long it takes you."

Bobbie seductively starts to unbutton her blouse exposing much cleavage of her breasts, drawing Richards attention.

"Oh, I see, I think I will learn much faster than I thought," says Richard with eyes staring at her breasts..

Richard pulls Bobbie over to him and continues to unbutton her blouse.

"Sweetheart, I kind of thought that you had beautiful breasts, but now that I see more of them, wow, I am in heaven!"

"Richard, they are all yours! What are you doing? Oh, you little devil. You should unhook my bra. It will be much easier for you to cup them in your hands. Slow down and enjoy the scenery. Oh… mmm…mmm," moans Bobbie, as Richard removes her bra and dips his head to her breasts and begins to suckle her nipples with his lips.

"OK, lover boy, you have done your thing. Now it is my turn. Let me show you how I teach sex."

"What, you have been teaching sex?"

"No, silly; teaching only you. Now follow my directions."

"Oh, I know what to do."

"Richard, be quiet," instructs Bobbie.

She lies down on the bed and pulls Richard over to her.

"Richard, climb over me and get on your knees. Now, move up and straddle my head with them, and grasp the headboard. Are you ready for the ride of your life, honey?"

Bobbie raises her head to his penis and gently places her lips around it and draws it into her mouth. Richard's penis swells as it lengthens. Bobbie starts to suck as she slowly moves her mouth up and down his shaft.

"Oh…oh..oh…, Bobbie, it feels good."

Bobbie releases his penis from her mouth and says, "Hold on, the ride has just started."

She, once again, engulfs his penis in her mouth and commences to draw it in and then out, steadily, each time a little faster. Richard starts to move in concert with the movements of her mouth.

"Mmmm..mmmm..oh, oh, Bobbie, I am going to 'cum'…"

Bobbie senses Richard's upcoming release as his penis hardens

4

more. Richard feels his release travel from his testicles up through to the tip of his penis, as Bobbie pulls for the last time. She grabs his penis and puts in between her breasts just as his release blasts out and spreads over them.

"Oh my God, Bobbie, what a ride, I must say!" Richard says panting.

"I told you the ride was going to be a blast. Now rub the semen around my breasts and over my nipples."

As Richard massages his semen around her breasts, the nipples enlarge and stand erect, inviting to suckle. He obliges with a general sucking, moving his tongue around and over them like a slow dance.

"Oh, ah..ah…mmm...mmm.," says Bobbie as she feels the wetness in her pussy increase.

"Honey, I am going to take you on a roller coaster ride. It is my turn," says Richard.

Bobbie starts to lift her hips up and then down in a rhythmic gesture. Richard starts kissing Bobbie's torso slowly down to her belly button, where he stops long enough for his tongue to dance in it. He gently places his hands on her inner thighs and pushes them out in a spreading motion. As he spreads her legs, Bobbie's lips of her pussy start to separate, and a slight discharge of her wetness is seen. He slowly alternates kisses on her inner thighs moving up to her love tunnel.

"Oh, Richard, I feel that I could 'cum' any moment."

"Hang on, honey, because we are just cresting the ride."

Bobbie anticipates his next move and readies herself, spreading her legs even farther. Richard nestles his face between her legs and pushes his face to her crotch and smells her. He is immediately aroused and sticks his tongue through her lips and into her pussy searching for her clit. Richard moves his tongue up, finding the target.

"Oh…oh…mmmm…mmm…ah…ahh……., I am 'cuming'," Bobbie desperately screams.

Richard moves his face so that he can insert a couple of fingers into her vagina. He reaches in search of the upper wall for the target.

His fingers find the mark, and he gently starts to move them in a circular motion with a consistent pressure.

"Richard, faster with more pressure. Ah…ah..yes…yes…yes… oh….ah…ah…yesssssssssss!"

Bobbie's 'cuming' reaches to a height she had not experienced before, while masturbating. The climaxing continues to rise to an unbearable height, but she still wants more.

"Richard, honey, I can hardly stand it, but I need more… ah..ah…mmm…"

In a short moment, Bobbie lets out a moan and then a scream as her wetness sprays out of her pussy and runs down to her ass.

"Honey, what did you do? It is an excruciating ecstasy. I want more…I want more!"

"It is your 'G' spot; your erogenous zone," Richard says as he once again reaches for the mark with his fingers.

"Ah,..ah…ah..yessss.yesss..mmm..mmm…"

Bobbie's body quivers and convulses as her wetness suddenly sprays out, once again, this time up Richard's arm to his shoulder.

Richard is so intense on pleasing Bobbie, he doesn't realize how hard is penis has gotten.

Bobbie looks at it and says, "Honey, put that big boy in and push it in deep. I want to feel all of you!"

Richard places the tip of his penis between the lips of her love tunnel and slowly enters. He pushes very gently until he feels the end. He withdraws and starts the motion again. Bobbie feels him swell inside her as he thrusts.

"Fuck me. Fuck me, honey!"

He thrusts faster, and he can feel the fluid build and climb to its exit as he releases. Bobbie feels a sudden warmth as his release makes it target in her vagina. Richard slowly lowers himself on Bobbie as both of their bodies quiver from excitement. He brushes her hair from her face and gently places his hands on each side of her head and pushes his face to her as their lips meet with a passionate kiss. Bobbie twists her tongue with Richard's.

As he slides off her and rolls to her side, he feels a slight resistance as his penis pulls out of her vagina, slowly releasing its grip.

After a moment of silence, Bobbie says, with her body still quivering and slight numbness in her vagina, "Richard, my sweetheart, that was a wild ride! I want more......"

DOUBLE TROUBLE

A typical Wednesday night at the gym and trouble is lurking.

"Hey, Ron, isn't that the chick who has the tight looking ass?" asks Mike.

"Oh, my God, it is! I have had a hard-on for her ever since we were at that restaurant," says Ron.

"Yeah, I would love to get some of that pussy, too," says Mike.

"I heard that she killed her husband," states Ron.

"Yeah, he tried to kill her first. He was a psychopath! I bet she fucked him so hard it drove him to lunacy! Bring it on!" exclaims Mike.

"Listen, Mike. I am going to find a way to that bitch's cunt. You watch me!"

"How are you going to do that, Ron? She is the Chief of Police, now, ya know?"

"I don't care if she is the Mother Mary, she has what I want! Later, I will fill you in later of how I am going to fuck her. Let's get over there and watch her ass go through those gyrations. I feel the need for a stiff one," says Ron.

"Bobbie, look at those guys over there?"

"Yeah, I see, Julia. Why are they staring at us?"

"They are usually over there watching the teenage girls perform their workout routines. They are the two guys who came into the restaurant while Tim and I were having dinner. The guys I told you about making remarks about my ass. Watch out for them! They are up to no good. We only have about fifteen minutes left to our workout, and then we can get out of here," states Julia.

"Mike, when that brunette babe comes out of this gym entrance door, be ready to slip the blindfold over her eyes."

"Ron, she won't just stand there while I do that."

"Of course not, you dick! Force her against the wall and detain her by holding her arm behind her back. If she squirms, push her arm up into her back. She will stop squirming, and I will be there to help. The most important thing is that she does not see our faces," states Ron.

"What do we do with the other chick who is with her?" asks Mike.

"I have been watching how they leave the gym after their routines, and the redhead goes out the other gym entrance. They never leave together."

"Ron, I kind of like that redheaded chick."

"What is it about her?" asks Ron.

"She appears to be young….and I'll bet that she has a nice and tight snatch…"

"That is your problem, Mike. My attention is on that brunette with the ass that is inviting me to penetrate it."

"So, Ron, what are you going to do to her, and here?"

"Just watch, Mike, just watch."

"Good night Julia; that was a great workout! I feel those carbs burning."

"Yup, Bobbie, I will see you next Wednesday night?"

"Oh, yes, I wouldn't miss it for anything."

"Say hello to Richard for me."

"Julia!"

"Oh Bobbie, come on! You know I don't have feelings for your husband; never did."

"Yeah, I know, Julia. I am just kidding."

JULIA'S ASSAULT

As Julia swings the gym entrance door open to travel to her car.

"Hey, bitch!" Mike presses Julia's body to the wall with her arm pinned behind her back.

"Quick, get that blindfold on her!" orders Ron.

"I am trying; I am trying. This cunt is strong!"

"Here, press her arm in and upward. She will stop fighting it, You, lady, are strong. I love a strong woman. I'll bet you are strong down...," Ron says as Julia interrupts.

"Who are you?" Julia asks.

"Never mind bitch," Ron states.

"You and I are going to have some fun. Come on, honey, walk," orders Ron.

"You don't know who you are messing with," states Julia.

"I don't give a damn who you are. I am going to get a piece of your ass, and you are going to love it!" Ron exclaims.

"Put a gag in her mouth; I don't want to hear any more of her talk, just her moans as I penetrate her sweet pussy," Ron instructs.

"Bend over, bitch. Lay down on the hood of the car! Hold her down!" Ron shoots orders to Mike.

"Are you going to do it here?" questions Mike.

"Oh, yeah, my cock is throbbing for her pussy. Now yank those Spandex® britches down!" orders Ron.

Mike grabs Julia's pants and proceeds to pull them down exposing her bare ass.

Ron ganders at Julia's pussy; almost 'cums' before penetrating her. Ron steps forward to Julia's ass and lifts his stiff cock to line it up with her vagina. Just as he is about to thrust and penetrate her, Julia lifts her leg and lets out a reverse kick square to Ron's groin.

"Oh, shit, it is so excruciating!" screams Ron as he hits the ground on his knees. "I think I am bleeding!" screams Ron.

"Quick, grab her!" exclaims Ron.

Mike grabs Julia as she is pulling up her Spandex® pants. He forces her face to the hood of the car.

"Oh, oh, I am hurting," screams Ron.

"Tie her hands behind her back!" Ron could hardly speak the order.

"Do you think that if we tie her feet, we could have another go at it?" asks Mike.

"Look, tie her hands and let the cunt go. I can't even get up from the ground. I am shot!" states Ron.

"Yeah, but I am not, and I would like a piece of her ass!" says Mike.

"Leave her and let's get out of here, now help me up. Oh, oh, it is painful to walk. I will get you, bitch! You won't get away with this!" yells Ron.

THE ESCAPE

Julia manages to roll off the hood of the car and land softly on the ground. She scoots herself over to the driver's side door and slowly stands up. She maneuvers herself to the rear-view mirror and manages to hook the rope around her hands on the mirror. Slowly, but deliberately, she loosens the knot on the rope, and her hands are free. Julia removes her blindfold and looks around her surroundings trying to see the men who assaulted her. There was no one in sight. Julia composes herself and, just for a moment, wonders if the guy penetrated her. She doesn't recognize the familiar feeling of her vagina, after penetration, like she was so used to when she and Tim would make love. There was no discharge from her vagina and no wet spots on her Spandex® pants, so she was assured that he did not get off in her.

Shaken up, Julia finds her car and drives to her apartment. As soon as Julia opens the door to her apartment, she strips her clothes off as she hurries to the shower. After the long shower, she lies down on her bed thinking about what had just happened to her and calls Bobbie.

"Hi, Bobbie!"

"What's wrong Julia? You sound terrible!" exclaims Bobbie.

"Do you have time to come over here? I need to talk to you."

"Sure, Julia, Richard is watching the game on the TV; he won't miss me."

"Richard, I am going over to see Julia. Something is wrong. I will return as soon as I can," states Bobbie.

"OK, baby, I hope everything is OK with Julia. I love you!" says Richard.

"I love you too, honey!" responds Bobbie.

REFLECTIONS

B obbie rushes over to Julia's apartment.

"Hello, is that you, Bobbie?" Julia asks, when a knock is heard at her apartment door.

"Yes, Julia, it is me."

"Hold on while I unlock the door."

"Julia, where did you get those bruises on your arms and, looks like rope burns around your wrists? Oh, honey, your face is bruised as well. Let me wipe those tears from your eyes."

"I was attacked; assaulted, Bobbie."

"Where, when, Julia?"

"As I was leaving the gym tonight after our workout routines, I was shoved against the wall at the entrance door with my arm pulled tightly to my back. They blindfolded me and dragged me over to a car and shoved my face onto the hood. One of them pulled my Spandex® pants down to expose my ass. I don't know, but I believe I was just seconds from penetration from the other one. I lifted my leg and kicked back to his groin. That stopped him from going further while the other one tied my wrists. I was able to get the rope on my wrist untied with cleverness on the mirror of the car. When I removed the blindfold, I could see no one in the area. They must have fled fast. I rushed back here and took a shower."

"Oh, my God, Julia! Do you think it was those two guys in the gym that gawk at us?"

"I don't know, Bobbie. I didn't recognize their voices."

"Julia, you were so close to being raped. I take that back. You were raped!"

"No, Bobbie, I was sexually assaulted. There was no penetration, but I had to think for a while whether I was or whether I wasn't. It all happened so fast."

"Is there any chance for DNA testing?" asks Bobbie.

"No, I didn't find any semen on my Spandex® or the ground. The one who had his penis out was lying on the ground moaning after I kicked him. He said that he was bleeding, but I did not see any blood anywhere. I don't think he got off and I don't think he will get off, any time soon, where I kicked him," states Julia.

"What are you going to do, Julia?"

"I don't know. I am still a bit shaken up from all of this."

RON'S FAILURE

Ron and Mike return to the bar to have a few drinks.

"Mike, I should have known that bitch would pull a stunt like that. After all, she is a cop. Man, does my dick hurt!"

"Ron, I guess you will be out of commission for a while. Do you think that she knows who we are?"

"Not a chance, there is no way. We will continue to frequent the gym on Wednesday nights when she is there. She will be less likely to suspect it was us," says Ron.

"Yeah, Ron, but we must concentrate on those teen chicks."

"No, way, Mike! We continue to watch her. If we stop watching her routine, she will suspect. We have to think like cops."

"Sure, Ron, like you did when you were within inches of having your way with her."

"It doesn't matter, we will still watch her; hell, I may be hurting in my crotch, but I still want her, and I will get her. I need to devise another plan."

SEX AS A WEAPON

C hief Lillus picks up the receiver to her phone to make a call.

"Richard and Bobbie, would you please come into my office?" asks Chief Lillus.

"OK, we have a possible homicide over in Cloverville. From what I gather a woman, there, murdered her husband. It isn't determined, but it appears it is what happened. I need you two to go over to the home. The address is 456 Huntington. The local police are over there now, and are asking our assistance."

"Hi, my name is Deputy Richard Peltz and this is my partner, Deputy Bobbie Fritz. We are from the Harford Police Department."

"Hello, my name is Officer Jones, and this is Inspector Roberts."

"Where is the body?" asks Officer Fritz.

"In the bathroom; in the bedroom, his wife is in there too," responds Officer Jones.

"What are you getting from her?" asks Officer Peltz.

"Nothing! She isn't talking. She just weeps," states Inspector Roberts.

"Any indication that she murdered her husband," asks Officer Fritz.

"No, she is not showing any emotion that would lead us to the fact," replies the Inspector.

"Who called the murder in?" asks Officer Peltz.

"She did," replies Officer Jones.

"Officer Fritz will go and try to talk to her. Fritz works with difficult personalities and family conflicts," states Officer Peltz.

"Be my guest," replies Inspector Roberts.

OFFICER **BOBBIE FRITZ** ENTERS THE BEDROOM AND SEES A WOMAN
SITTING ON A BED CRYING

"Hello, my name is Officer Fritz from the Harford Police Department. You can call me Bobbie if you would like. I want to discuss with you what happened, here. What is your name?"

"It's Vivian, Vivian Lewis."

"Is it OK if I call you Vivian?"

"Yes, you can," replies Vivian.

"Here, let me wipe those tears for you and here are some tissues," says Officer Fritz.

"Vivian, can you remember what happened? Where is the body?"

"He is over there in the bathroom," Vivian points.

Officer Fritz walks over to the bathroom and opens the door.

"Oh, damn, what the hell?" she exclaims.

She examines closer and recognizes the body of a male, nude, with his throat slit. Blood is all over the bathroom floor. Officer Fritz quickly grabs a towel and places it over his genitals.

"Please take Vivian to the other room," she directs Officer Jones.

"Officer Peltz, please come in here to the bathroom."

As soon as Richard enters the bathroom, he sees Bobbie sobbing.

"Bobbie, what is wrong? Do you recognize the body?"

Bobbie nods, "Yes Richard. Look over there on the wall behind the shower curtain."

"Holy, shit! What the hell…Bobbie it is a picture of you and shit, he ejaculated all over your face! Who the hell is he?"

"He is one of those two guys who has been eying Julia and me when we go to the gym for our workouts. They had made remarks to Julia and Tim, when he was alive, but never about me that I know."

"How the hell did he get a picture of you, Bobbie?"

"Probably with his cell phone, I would guess. I must question Vivian. I know the picture is part of the crime scene, Richard, but please remove it and place it face down on the counter. Oh, and Richard, please remove the ejaculate…I am sorry honey."

"Vivian, who is that person lying on the floor in your bathroom?" asks Officer Fritz.

"It is my husband, Mike; Mike Lewis."

"How did he get there? Did you hurt him?"

"My husband Mike, has been a stalker ever since I have known him. I should have divorced him a long time ago. I did not know how bad he had gotten chasing woman. He and his friend would go to the gym every Wednesday night to supposedly workout."

"What gym is that, Vivian?"

"It is the Silver Lining Gym in Harford."

"How is it Mike is lying there with his throat slit?" asks Officer Fritz.

"I heard Mike the other night talking to his friend over the phone. They were discussing something about a woman at the gym."

"What did he say about the woman at the gym?"

"Well, he…I don't want to say."

"Please, Vivian, I need to hear all of the details."

"They would go to the gym and stalk the young teenage girls, but this one night, it sounded like they were stalking a woman."

"Vivian, what did Mike say to his friend over the phone?"

"Well, he said something like, he told his friend that he about had it stalking those young teenage girls and wanted some real pussy. He said he wanted the mature kind."

"Did he say anything else?"

"Yeah, he told his friend that he was going to fuck this woman at the gym the first chance that he had, and sometime soon, he would do it. It sounded like maybe his friend tried something but failed."

"Vivian, did you hear when and how Mike was going to do this, and to what woman?"

"Not in the conversation, but from what I heard from other phone conversations, Mike described a woman, maybe in her mid-twenties, redheaded and beautiful, much like you. He said that her ass, or moves, gave him a hard-on."

"Do you know what Mike's friend's name is?" asks Officer Fritz.

"No, I never got wind of it in any phone conversations that I had heard."

"Vivian, did you look at the picture on the wall of the shower?"

"No, it is disgusting what he did on that picture."

"So, you do not recognize the picture of the woman?"

"No, I couldn't look. It is too disgusting. Poor thing! If she only knew what she was up against if the picture is of the woman Mike was talking about fucking. Oh, well, it is over now…she is safe."

"Vivian, how did Mike get his throat cut?"

"Mike came home from the gym last night, and he was real horny acting. He wanted to get 'laid' and forced me to have sex with him. He was rough with me and made my vagina bleed."

"It sounds to me, Mike raped you, Vivian."

"Can a guy rape his wife? We are married…"

"Vivian, any forcible sex act without consent is rape. Your husband raped you. What happened next?"

"He was very tired after fucking me and fell asleep. I tried to sleep, but I was in too much pain down there, ya know? At about two in the morning, I heard the shower running and noticed that Mike was not in bed. I figured that he was taking a shower. When the shower was turned off, I heard Mike moaning. I thought that he might have fallen and hurt himself, so I got out of bed and went to the bathroom door. I opened the door and...dear God, I can't..."

"Vivian, it is OK. Describe to me what you saw."

"He was behind the shower curtain moving around and moaning. I pulled open the shower curtain and, oh..."

"Go on, Vivian."

"He was standing there with his hand around his penis and moaning while he was rubbing it."

"Do you mean he was masturbating?"

"Yes, and all of a sudden he ejaculated on the tub enclosure wall."

"Just the wall?"

"Yes, but on the wall was a picture of this woman...that bastard, he was disgusting...he...he ejaculated on that woman's face."

"Vivian, can you tell me anything about what the woman in the picture looked like?"

"I remember, she was a redhead and beautiful. Like I said; just like you."

"What happened next, Vivian?"

--As Vivian opens the bathroom door, she sees the shower curtain closed.

"Mike, are you OK? Why are you moaning?"

Vivian opens the shower curtain.

"Mike, what the hell? You are a disgusting bastard!"

"Well, bitch, it is more than you give me and much prettier, too."

"Mike, I give you sex anytime you want it, and you did get it tonight, forcibly, I might add."

"Yeah, every time I get 'laid' by you, I see in my mind, this redhead's cunt, while thrusting my dick. Why do you think that I 'cum' so easily? It isn't because I visualize you in my mind...far from it!"

"Mike, you are disgusting! I knew your stalking would someday lead to this, but not that I would see it."

"Well, stick around, because I am going to drag that bitch here and I am going to force you to watch while I fuck her!"

"Mike, I am going to call the police. You have lost your mind, and I am scared."--

---

"I ran to the kitchen to the phone, and Mike chased after me."

--"Oh no you don't, bitch! You aren't calling anyone. Get into the bedroom and lie down on the bed."

"No, Mike, I am too sore! My vagina is bleeding. No Mike, no more sex!"

"Where did you get that knife, Mike?"

"Never mind. I have it just in case you squirm. Now, take those panties off, or I will cut them off!"

"No, Mike, no! Mike, get off me. You are hurting me!"--

"What happened next?" asks Officer Fritz.

"I lifted my legs and Mike fell back onto the floor. The knife fell out of his hand onto the bed next to me, so I picked it up."

--"All right, bitch, I have had about enough of you! I am going to cut you! Give me that knife!"

"No Mike, don't you dare get back on top of me."

"I will get back on top of you if I want, now, spread those legs!"

"No, Mike, I will not!"

"Fine, I will enter you from the back, now roll over!"—

———

"Vivian, was it at this point when Mike's throat was slit?" asks Officer Fritz.

"Mike came to the bed and pushed me onto my stomach. He lifted my hips while on his knees on the bed. He was ready to penetrate me from behind. I lifted my hand with the knife and tried to cut him to stop. As soon as I lifted my hand, I lost my balance, and my knees buckled. Mike fell on me, and the knife must have been in the right position. The next thing I know, Mike lifted off me holding his neck. Blood was dripping through his fingers as he went into the bathroom. Mike fell on the floor. I stayed sitting on the bed just as you seen me when you entered the bedroom. I, of course, put my panties back on and my housecoat."

"Vivian, you need to go to the hospital."

"No, I am OK, he didn't enter me this time."

"No, I don't mean for that. You are bleeding. Look at your panties."

———

"Officer Peltz, please call an ambulance," states Officer Fritz.

"Vivian needs to go to the emergency room."

"Inspector Roberts, I have all of the information I need and will get the report to you first thing in the morning. Vivian does not need to be cuffed or under police surveillance. Get the Coroner over here to pick up the body. We have completed our work, here," says Officer Fritz.

LOVERS

R ichard and Bobbie step out of the Lewis house and get into
their squad car.

"Bobbie, I don't necessarily like to refer to you as Officer Fritz."

"Oh, Richard, what would you rather call me?"

"Well, the first thing is to recognize you are my wife, so, I guess the second thing that comes to mind is 'Sex Goddess.'"

"Richard, you animal! I suppose this means that you are feeling a little frisky? You want a little T&A tonight, huh?"

"Yup, you got it, baby. The 'roller coaster' for you," says Richard amorously.

"I hate to burst your preemptive orgasm, Richard, but while we are on duty, you are Officer Peltz, and I am Officer Fritz."

"Yeah, I know, but in my head, I am referring you to be my 'Sex Goddess.'"

"OK, OK, Richard, you can dream about getting 'laid' all you want, but we need to report back to Julia."

JUSTICE IS SERVED

R ichard and Bobbie return to the office to tell Chief Lillus of their findings.

"Chief, I mean Julia, we went to the home of the murder victim, and you won't believe what unfolded," says Bobbie.

"Were you able to decipher who murdered the man?" asks Julia.

"I got one better. Do you remember the guy or guys at the gym who gawk at us while we work out at the gym?"

"Yeah, what about them, Bobbie?"

"Well, the guy who was murdered; his name is Mike Lewis, the blonde guy of the two," says Bobbie.

"How did you find that out?"

"He was married to a woman named Vivian. She told me that Mike and his friend would go to the gym on Wednesday nights to gawk at the teenage girls. It is the same gym we visit. His wife knew that he was a stalker. Anyway, after he forcibly raped her, he took a shower, and she discovered he was getting off in front of a picture of a woman affixed to the shower stall wall."

"He was doing this in the shower? What a disgusting pig! How are you sure this Mike Lewis is one of the guys stalking us?" asks Julia.

"I was able to see him up close when he opened the entrance door to the gym, while I exited one night. He has a scar on his right cheek running from his temple to his jaw, probably from a fight. The body murdered had the same scar."

"Good work, Bobbie, is there anymore?"

"Yes, that disgusting bastard spewed his juice all over the picture of this woman's face."

"Did you recognize the woman in the picture?" asks Julia.

"Sure did, it is a picture of me."

"Holy shit! Really, Bobbie?"

"Yes!"

"So, the wife killed him?" asks Julia.

"Yes, he was angered she saw him ejaculating on the picture. He tried to rape her again . He had a knife, and she got a hold of it. When she pushed him away, he fell and slit his own throat."

"Self-defense, I would say," states Julia.

"Julia, do you think this Mike Lewis or his friend was the one who tried to rape you?"

"It is hard to say, Bobbie. This Mike seemed to be content on spewing on your picture. If his friend has a picture of me and ejaculating on it, more power to him. At least we only have one gawking at us, now. Go ahead and write up the report. Inspector Roberts wants the details. Where is Vivian Lewis, now?"

"She was taken to the emergency room by ambulance. Mike Lewis ruffed her up badly and did some damage to her vagina. The Coroner has the body of the murder victim."

"Good work, Bobbie! This case is wrapped up!"

SICK BASTARD

The teenage girls at the gym are in conversation as Ron steps in.

"Hey, Ronnie baby, where is your friend?" asks one of the teenage girls at the gym.

"I am going to miss him staring at my ass tonight while I work out; maybe in and out……"

"Yeah, it is a good thing you are under age because if you weren't, I would be fucking you!" exclaims Ron.

"In and out, Ronnie baby, any time!"

THE RAPE

J ulia picks up her phone to call Bobbie.

"Hey, Bobbie, I am not feeling well tonight. I am going to have to take a rain check on my work out," says Julia.

"I am sorry, Julia. That's OK; I will go by myself. I will be back before you know it. Can I get you anything while I am out?"

"No, Bobbie, but thanks, and hey Bobbie?"

"Yes."

"Be careful. We still have one stalker. I don't trust him. Don't get cornered."

"OK, Julia, I am a cop, you know."

"Yeah, Bobbie, I am a cop too and almost died."

"I am sorry Julia. I didn't intend it to come out that way."

"Hey, have fun Bobbie. Next week I will have to have a double calorie burn."

BOBBIE IS ALMOST FINISHED WITH HER WORK OUT WHEN SHE NOTICES THE STALKER IS NO LONGER STANDING WHERE SHE HAD JUST SEEN HIM

"Well, hopefully, he got bored and left. Good riddance" mutters Bobbie.

"Here, let me open the door for you."

A voice came from out of the darkness at the gym entrance door where Bobbie leaves to go back to her home.

"Well, thank you," says Bobbie.

She steps out through the entrance door and is grabbed from behind. Her hands are put behind her back, and she is handcuffed. She is blindfolded and forced to the ground. The attacker places shackles on her ankles.

"I got you, bitch! You were Mikes cunt, but because he isn't here, you are my cunt tonight. I am not going to be brutal like I normally am. I ask you, how do you want it? Frontal, doggy style, ruff and forcibly? I will do any one of them you pick, or any combination if you so desire."

"None of them, you bastard," says Bobbie.

"Now is that the way to treat a gentleman?"

"You are no gentleman. You are a pervert! I can't see you, but I know you are the one is stalking my friend and me."

"Oh yes, your friend. Are you referring to that cunt with the long black hair? The one who has the ass I almost fucked?"

"You! So you were the one. I should have guessed!"

"And you, my little bitch, are the one Mike took a picture and got off on. Guess what? I have the real thing. Now, how do you want it, or do I decide for you?"

"You will never get away with this."

"Oh, and what are you going to do about it? You seem to be all tied up now! Times up! We are going to go to the ballet practice area, and I am going to undo your blindfold so you can watch."

"You are a sick bastard."

"Oh, look here, they must be using this room as a storage area while they renovate the gym. We have a vaulting horse over here. Now bend over, bitch!"

Bobbie reluctantly bends over the horse with force from her attacker. Ron ties Bobbie down so she cannot rise from the apparatus.

"There, sweetheart, with the mirrors you have the perfect view of me fucking your ass! Oh, you aren't able to pull your Spandex® pants down, so I will do it for you."

Bobbie starts to scream.

"Stop your screaming. No one can hear you over the loud music playing in the gym; but not to distract from the moment, I will place a gag in your mouth."

Bobbie twists her head back and forth to avert Ron placing the gag in her mouth.

"Hold on, bitch," says Ron as he grabs her long red hair and steadies her head.

"No, no; stop! No...no...no....," Bobbie's screams are muffled as the gag is put in place.

"OK, sweetie, I think I am ready! The anticipation of seeing your sweet pussy will get me hard as a rock."

Bobbie starts kicking her legs but is limited due to the shackles on her ankles.

"I bet you don't know why I shackled your ankles, do ya? The reason is so that you can't kick me as that bitch did to me...what's her name? Julia, I believe. Oh, one last thing. I need to tie your ankles to the supports on this apparatus, so you can't flail them, and to keep those beautiful legs of yours open for my entrance. If you will only cooperate, this can be over sooner."

Bobbie screams a muffled scream and tries to squirm out of her predicament.

"OK honey," Ron says as he places his hands on her hips and pulls her Spandex® pants down to her knees.

"Oh, God, what a sight! Your ass looks sweeter than what I could have ever imagined. I usually don't take long, but honey, this time, I am going to take my time."

Bobbie feels the tears welling in her eyes as she starts to feel him penetrate her. She moans, but not of ecstasy, but in sorrow.

"See, honey, it doesn't hurt. I am very gentle with my thrusting. After all, I don't want to damage your pussy. I will be visiting it again."

For a moment, Bobbie becomes unconscious. When she comes to, his thrusting continues, and she is feeling very raw. Her vagina is getting numb from the loss of her wetness, which is not flowing, due to not being aroused.

"Ah, ah, oh, my load is exploding….oh, oh feel that honey? Feel my load?"

Suddenly, she feels the familiar warmth she feels when Richard ejaculates into her vagina. She cries endlessly and vomits profusely.

Ron withdraws his penis from Bobbie's vagina and watches as his 'cum' runs down her ass onto the floor.

"All done, bitch! I wish I had time to go another round with you, but it can wait. There will be other times. Maybe by the third or fourth time, we won't need all these shackles. What do you have to say about that?"

———

Bobbie, still gagged, moans and is in a full cry. She could see in the mirror his thrusting into her bare ass. When she closes her eyes, the vivid picture of him penetrating her is reflected in her retinas. She thinks of Richard and how she will be able to explain this to him to convince him that it wasn't her fault.

———

"I am going to unshackle you, but keep you gagged and your hands in cuffs, and oh, I will pull your Spandex® pants back up over your ass. Someone will find you, and then you can get free from the rest of the restraints. I highly suggest you don't tell anyone about our little encounter. I will be around, but no one will recognize me, even you until we meet again. You will learn to love our interludes. After all, I do give good sex, don't I? Next time we will try to get some pleasure for you. I am sorry about that, but I needed to make my tracks first. You know what I mean."

"See you around honey, and oh, don't call me. I will find you for our next 'in and outing'."

THE RESCUE

A few hours pass and there is a rustling at the ballet room door.

"Holy crap! What the hell happened in here? Here, let me remove the gag from your mouth."

"Please, unshackle my ankles," says Bobbie. "Please remove these cuffs from my wrists."

"But I don't have a key."

"Pull my Spandex® pants cuff up, and you will see a garter around my leg, just below my left knee."

"Oh, no ma'am, I can't touch you, oh, no."

"Look, what has just happened to me is more than you can ever do. There are keys in the garter. One of them should work."

"OK ma'am, remember, you asked me to touch you. I am not accustomed to touching a woman's bare skin of whom I do not know."

"Don't worry, you are not raping me. I am so grateful for your help."

"Hey, these keys work. How come you have keys to your shackles? I better call the police. It looks as if someone had their way with you."

"Yes, they did, and I must go."

"I need to call the police!"

"Young man, I am a cop. Thank you so much, and I apologize that you have to clean this mess up."

"Jeesh, it looks like semen."

"It is, and I am sorry," says Bobbie.

"You were......, or someone had see...x with you?" asks the rescuer.

<hr>

BOBBIE DOES NOT ANSWER HIS QUESTION. SHE IS ON HER WAY TO THE EMERGENCY ROOM

<hr>

"Hi, my name is Police Officer Peltz, Bobbie Peltz. I need to see a doctor right away!" states Bobbie.

"Why are you here, ma'am?" asks the nurse.

"I need to see a doctor right away. I hope it isn't too late."

"Too late for what?" asks the nurse.

"I need a rape kit!"

"OK, OK, I will get the doctor right away."

<hr>

"I am doctor Linda Perez. I understand you would like a rape kit? You married Ms....?"

"Mrs. Peltz, Bobbie Peltz."

"Who raped you if I may ask?"

"I don't know. He blindfolded me," as Bobbie starts to tear up.

"He violated me..ohhhhh."

"Mrs. Peltz, after I take care of you, it is in your best interest to get some counseling to help you cope with the violation done to you."

"I think I will be all right in a few days."

"Mrs. Peltz, you might be in denial. Sometimes it takes a little bit of time after a rape before it sets into your mind. I will need to look inside, Mrs. Peltz. It will be a little uncomfortable. Just relax," says the nurse.

"Mrs. Peltz, your vagina looks OK. There is no tearing of the lining and no blood. The rape kit should stop a pregnancy, so don't worry about it. When was your last period?"

"I just finished my period yesterday," says Bobbie.

"I am also prescribing a battalion of antibiotics in case you contracted any STD's. You should be OK, but you will need therapy. You may not think you need it now, but as I said, when the encounter hits your mind, you will need it. Be patient; it takes some time to get mentally back to normal, if ever," says Dr. Perez.

"Thank you, doctor Perez."

NICOLE

J ulia steps into the doorway of Bobbie's cubicle.

"Bobbie, will you please step into my office?" asks Chief Lillus.

"Julia, what's up?" asks Bobbie.

"We have a strange case. A couple of girls at the gym called in to the office worried about a guy who hasn't been to the gym for a couple of weeks."

"Don't tell me the girls are teenagers."

"I do not know, Bobbie. I haven't heard about a missing person from anyone else. I am going to go to the gym this afternoon and see what I can find out. Meanwhile, you can go around and canvas the local businesses and see if anyone is missing a regular."

"OK, Julia, I am on it."

"We will convene a little later today and discuss our findings, and Bobbie, take your hubby with you."

JULIA ENTERS THE GYM AND WALKS OVER TO THE TEENAGE GIRLS

"Hey, girls," says Julia.

"I recognize you. Wednesday nights, right?" says one of the teenage girls.

"Yes, you are correct. My name is Chief Julia Lillus of the Harford Police Department."

"A cop? Who would have known."

"A couple of calls have been sent to my office concerning a missing person. A male from this gym? Did any of you girls make the calls?" asks Julia.

"I made one of those calls," said one of the girls.

"What is your name?" asks Julia.

"I am Nicole."

"Tell me about your concern."

"A guy who always shows up on Wednesday nights has not been here for a couple of weeks."

"Who is this guy and what relation is he to you?"

"You know. You have seen him. He always watches us with his friend. I see him staring at your ass during your routine."

"I am pretty sure I know who you are referring to? What relation is he to you?" asks Chief Lillus.

"He is no relation to any of us, but he watches our asses, too, during our workouts. His name is Ron. I call him Ronnie baby," says Nicole.

"It sounds as if you are friends with this Ron," says Chief Lillus.

"Yeah, I am, and I am quite pissed that he hasn't shown up to watch my ass," says Nicole.

"Why is that, Nicole?"

"Because he threatens to fuck me."

"You are angered because he is making sexual advances to you, yet you miss him? I do not understand," says the Chief.

"No, I want him to follow through with his threat. I want him to fuck me, and he hasn't yet! I keep asking him to do it, but he won't. I want him back, so he will make good with his threat."

"Nicole, how old are you?" asks Chief Lillus.

"I just turned sixteen yesterday," says Nicole.

"You do realize you are underage, don't you?"

"Yeah, I could give a crap. I want him to fuck me!"

"Listen to me, Nicole, and all you girls, too. Stay away from Ron and any other man who approaches you! You may think it is cool that they are looking at your asses while you are working out, but that kind of thinking will get you into trouble and maybe even harm you in some way, let alone getting you pregnant. Now, when was the last time you saw Ron, here?" asks Chief Lillus.

"It has been exactly two weeks from today," Nicole says.

"Thank you, girls, for the information. Remember what I told you, especially you, Nicole! You are not ready for sex at your age. There is no contest in losing your virginity. Save it for the one you will love someday!" states Chief Lillus..

TEENAGE GIRLS AND CONDOMS

B obbie returns to the office to talk to Julia.

"Bobbie, what did you find out about the missing person?" asks Julia.

"A couple of drugstores told me that a certain male, who regularly visits to buy condoms, hasn't been in for a couple of weeks. They are quite sure he is single, and they never seen anyone with him when in their store," says Bobbie.

"Well, Bobbie, I found who the missing person is. The other male stalker at the gym is our guy. I learned his name is Ron. The teenage girls at the gym are the ones who called into our office. One of them, named Nicole, knows of him very well. She insisted that she wanted Ron to enter into sex with her! She says he threatens to have sex with here all the time. He probably won't do it because he knows she and the other girls are all underage. What the hell is wrong with these young girls nowadays?"

"Wow, the stalking is more serious than we thought," says Bobbie.

"What is our next move, Julia?"

"We wait and see if any clues come our way. I am in no hurry to get him back!" exclaims Julia.

"Me neither! Buying condoms weekly with no wife or supposed girlfriend. I wonder where he uses them?" says Bobbie.

"Those teenage girls may be more involved with him than they indicate," says Julia.

———

Bobbie goes back to her office and sits at her desk thinking about the rape. "Ron certainly didn't use a condom when he raped me," she mutters. "I bet those girls are giving away their virginity to that bastard."

———

SEX IS DEAD FOR RICHARD

R ichard steps into the kitchen of his home and faces Bobbie.

"Hey, Bobbie can we talk about something?" asks Richard.

"Sure, honey, what is on your mind?"

"Come and sit next to me."

"OK."

"Do you remember how hot our erotic sexual episodes were when we were first married?"

"Yes, Richard, I do. How can I forget?"

"Well, Bobbie, I feel that you have forgotten. We haven't had one of those sessions for the past several weeks."

"Richard, I am sorry. I just have been under the weather lately. We will get back there sometime."

"Bobbie, the only sex we have had lately, is foreplay. You do not want penetration, and you don't even want to touch my penis. Bobbie, I miss you….I miss your body! You have told me that you are going to some counseling. Is that why you are shunning me?"

"No, not at all, Richard, women tend to go to counseling now and then. You must have realized by now; females are complicated."

"I know, Bobbie. I am worried your love for me has diminished since we were first married."

"Oh, Richard, not at all! Come over here, sweetheart."

Bobbie pulls Richard to her and kisses him as passionate as she can.

RICHARD MUST BE TOLD

B obbie is full of anxiety going to the office today.

"Julia, I feel that I am losing Richard!"

"Why? How?" Julia asks.

"I can't get myself to have sex with him. Sure, we fondle each other in foreplay, but I don't feel comfortable for penetration. I can't even touch his penis."

"How are counseling sessions going? Are they helping with this?"

"Yes, but the rape dulled my feelings for sex. I love Richard, and I want to be available to him as a wife should. I do not want to lose him. I am afraid if I cannot get over this, he will go."

"Bobbie, does he not understand what the rape has done to your sexual desires?"

"Julia, I have not told him about the rape."

"What? He needs to know in order to understand. It is the only way to keep him. I do believe that he is man and husband enough to deal with it. He won't leave you because of the rape. Isn't he supposed to be counseling with you?"

"He is supposed to go to the counseling for husbands of raped woman," says Bobbie.

"He can't do this if he doesn't know, can he? Bobbie, you are going to have to tell him about the rape, soon. I say tonight. Devote the entire night for it and share your emotions. Make sure you cry together and hold each other."

"OK Julia, you are correct."

"Richard, when we get home from the office tonight, let's spend time together. Leave the television off; take the phone off the hook. Just you and I!"

"Sounds great to me. Finally!"

"Richard, try not to get your hopes set too high."

"OK, we can work into it," say Richard.

RICHARD AND BOBBIE ARRIVE HOME AND FINISH THEIR DINNER

"That was a very nice dinner you made tonight Bobbie."

"I am glad you liked it. I had you in mind when I made it. Now come over with me and sit next to me on the sofa. Please place your hand in mine," says Bobbie.

"I like this, Bobbie."

"Richard, hold my hand. Do you remember, about a month ago, on a Wednesday night when Julia was ill and couldn't accompany me to the gym?"

"Yes, I do. You were late coming home from the gym."

"Yes, Richard, there was a reason for my lateness."

"Bobbie, what is with the tears? You are trembling. What is wrong?"

"Hold me, Richard. I need you to hold me."

"OK."

"Honey, I was late that night because I was attacked on the way to my car to come home….oh…oh."

"Sweetheart, please don't tell me…."

"Yes, Richard, I was raped!" says Bobbie as she bursts into tears.

"Oh, honey, my sweetheart, move closer, let me hold you," says Richard as tears start to roll down his cheeks.

"I need to tell you the details, Richard, in order for me to sort it all out. I was blindfolded, handcuffed and shackles were placed on my ankles. I tried to get away, but he was very strong. He dragged me over to the ballet room and tied me down to a vaulting horse. Oh… oh…I am so sorry Richard….He pulled my Spandex® pants down, and he penetrated me. I was unconscious for a while, and when I came to, I could see him in the mirrors thrusting into my ass. I vomited as he continued to make me raw. He 'came' inside me….oh…oh..Richard, I am so sorry…I didn't ask for it, I swear."

"Bobbie, you poor dear, I do not think that you asked for it. It was not your fault."

"I should have had enough strength to get away."

"No, honey, no."

"Richard, you will probably never want to place your penis inside my vagina, again, now that another man has penetrated me with his semen."

"No, honey, that is not true."

"Richard you are the first man I have had sex with up until now. I waited just for you and now…oh…oh..I feel like such a whore!"

"No, sweetheart, you are not a whore. You are my beloved wife and I love you."

"Richard this is why I have been abstaining from having sex with you. I do not feel worthy, and I do not want you to enter into me where another man has been."

"Bobbie, I am so sorry. I did not know. I am so sorry I pushed you so much for sex."

"I am going to rape counseling to help me get past this. You can go to counseling for men to help you deal with my rape. Together we will get over this, and I promise when it happens our sex life will be very close to what it used to be."

"I know, Bobbie, it will be as it first was. I do not look down at you for this, and the rape does not hinder my feelings for you emotionally or physically. I love you, Bobbie! I yearn, even now, for the day I can enjoy your body…your entire body!"

"Hold me Richard and let's cry together."

"I am so sorry for you, Bobbie."

———

Richard and Bobbie never leave the sofa to go to their bed. They lie inclined holding each other tightly until morning.

———

SWEET REVENGE

T he next morning, Richard awakens before Bobbie.

"Good morning sweetheart," says Richard.

"Good morning honey, come here and kiss me. Richard, I have to tell you one more detail."

"What is it, sweetheart?"

"The guy who raped me is the other one of the two who is stalking Julia and me at the gym when we are performing our workouts; he is the one who made those remarks to Julia about her body in front of Tim during their dinner at the restaurant; he is the one who is most likely fucking the teenage girls at the gym; and lastly, he is the one who raped Julia at the gym."

"What? You never told me about Julia."

"She did not want anyone to know, besides she said she was not raped because she kicked him in the groin before he could penetrate her."

"How do you know it is this guy? Does Julia know it is this guy?"

"No, Julia doesn't know the man who raped, assaulted her, as being him. While I was being raped, he told me he was the one who assaulted her. He promised that he would get her again and finish the job."

"You need to tell Julia, don't you?"

"No, Richard, I cannot. This guy told me that he would be back to rape me again and again."

"What? That bastard! It isn't going to happen because I will be accompanying you wherever you go."

"There will be no need for that, Richard and what I am going to tell you is why we can never tell Julia who he is. We are going to kill him, Richard!"

"No way, we can't do that....but, how?"

"He wants my next interlude with him less restricting and hopes that I will reciprocate because I found I actually enjoyed it."

"I think I am going to vomit," says Richard.

"I will play his game, but it is crucial that you are there to help me stop him before he goes too far."

"How are we going to do that?"

"I have a plan," states Bobbie.

"What will we do with the body?"

"I have a plan for that as well. Look, Richard, I really don't want to do this because it is risky and from what I just went through, but it is the only way we can surely get to him," says Bobbie.

"Bobbie, it is not worth it if putting you at risk is the answer to getting him," states Richard.

"I have to do it...he must suffer and be done with," says Bobbie in response to Richard.

"Well, OK, let me hear your plan. But it does not mean I will agree going along with it!"

"The last thing he said to me was he would find me for another round of forced sex. He was presumptuous enough to suggest I should be more receptive the next time."

"That bastard!" shouts Richard.

"I need to take him up on his offer."

"Oh, no, no, Bobbie, no way!"

"Richard, you will be there, so he won't get very far before, you know, he is 'done away' with."

"I don't like this Bobbie!"

"Look, honey, it is the only way for sure we can lure him in order to kill him."

"Go on. I still don't like it."

"Calm down, sweetheart, you will see there will be no danger to me at all."

"How can you guarantee that? You say you will have to show your ass to him, again?"

"No, no, let me finish. He will need to get intoxicated first and this is where you come into the plan. You will go to the gym and meet him and brag to him about a woman who you fucked the other night in the ballet room. His interest will be perked because the ballet room is where he raped me, and I am sure it will be his place of choice, again. Richard, we have to make sure the timing is just right, so I do not get hurt!"

"Bobbie, I thought you said there would be no danger to you."

"There shouldn't be, honey, just be careful and remember the timing," says Bobbie.

RICHARD PLAYS THE PERVERT

R ichard enters the gym and finds Ron. He walks over to him.

"Hey, what a view over there! Look at those teenage girls moving their asses. It makes me hard watching them," Richard says.

"Yeah, you bet ya!" says Ron. "I come here every Wednesday evening to watch them. Hell, one of them...her, over there, actually wants me to fuck her," says Ron.

"Why don't you take her up on it?" asks Richard.

"I would, but she is only fifteen or sixteen years old and my ass would be thrown in jail, not that I wouldn't want to chance it to get into her pussy. She definitely is jail bait," says Ron.

"I think you should, although I prefer the older, more mature women to fuck. I have seen quite a few here lately," says Richard.

"Yeah, you know what? Every Wednesday evening there are these two chicks who come in for their workout routines and they are mature women. One is a brunette and the other is a short redhead. I took that brunette out to the parking lot one night and shoved my cock into her ass. Man, I get a hard on just visualizing her pussy; nice and tight. The redhead, on the other hand has a young and tight pussy that licks my shaft on every thrust. There is something to be said about a young pussy," boasts Ron.

"So, you fucked them both?" asks Richard.

"Yeah, but the redheaded bitch was a struggle. She was a live wire in the ballet room!" says Ron.

"Funny you mention the ballet room because I am very familiar with that room. I have fucked many in there. That vault horse. Bend over bitch!" says Richard.

"Yeah, you got that right!" Ron chimes in.

"Let's go out to the bar down the road and knock a few back as we discuss the details of the bitches we fucked," suggests Richard.

TOO MUCH TO DRINK

R ichard takes Ron down the road to the local bar.

"Waiter, please bring us a bottle of whiskey and two glasses," Richard requests.

"By the way, what is your name?" asks Ron.

"I am Rick; just call me Dick."

"Ha, ha, real clever," says Ron.

"OK, what do they call you?" asks Richard.

"My name is Ron, Ron Linden."

"Well, great Ron. Here, let me pour you a shot. So, tell me more about this redhead. I might want to try my luck with her," says Richard.

"Oh, no, she is mine. I made the tracks in her ass. You keep out!" exclaims Ron.

"OK OK, hang on there, I was only joking, but how about the brunette? How about I give her a try?" Richard suggests.

"Well, you can have one 'roll in the hay' with her, but don't make it a habit."

"Let's get back to the redhead. I need a hard on!" exclaims Richard.

"I pinned her over that vaulting horse and I sunk my cock deep into her pussy. You should have heard her moan. She actually loved it and asked for more."

"Why did you pin her to the horse? Here, take another shot of whiskey."

"As I said, she is a wild one and won't keep still. She promised that the next time we crossed paths, she would be easier for me to handle, although a bitch in bondage makes me harder," says Ron.

"Another shot, Ron?"

"Sure, why not? I am getting a little light headed. One more shot for the road."

"Let's get back to the gym. I want to watch some more teenage ass. I might even take up that bitch who wants to fuck. She won't tell anyone she is a minor; not as if she is not asking for it. Is she the one with the black Spandex® which are so tight when she bends over you can see her snatch as her ass moves with the background music?" asks Richard.

"Yup, that is her. You want to take a chance with her?" asks Ron.

"Yes, I think I will. I can feel her pussy calling for me," says Richard.

"Be sure to wear a condom. You don't want to get her pregnant!" exclaims Ron.

"Let me drive, Ron. You have had way too much to drink to drive."

BOBBIE PLAYS THE WHORE

R ichard and Ron return to the gym and immediately to search out the teenage girls.

"I am going over to that teenage chick right now."

"Wait a minute Dick. Look over there. The redhead I just told you about!"

"Are you sure, Ron?"

"I believe so. My head is a little fuzzy from that last shot of whiskey. Watch her routine, Dick, and tell me what you think of her."

"Wow, look at her ass!" exclaims Richard.

"I told you, Dick! Hey, let's both go to the ballet room with her. We can both fuck her, but I am first. I want to get her juiced up," says Ron.

"Sounds good to me. I guess I will just have to put the teenage chick on hold," says Richard disappointed.

"You won't regret it, Dick, the redhead is a real woman! Let's get over there and introduce ourselves."

"Hey, honey, remember me?"

"Yeah, I sure do, Ron. I saw you here earlier. My crotch is quite wet," states Bobbie.

"Well, now. You sure are thinking different from when we first met."

"You know, Ron, I was just playing hard to get. Like you said, I will want our next encounter, and here it is. Do you want to have your way with me tonight?" asks Bobbie.

"No fighting this time around?"

"No, Ron! I am going to take you up on what you told me. You are going to please me this time...as in getting me to 'cum'?"

"Yes, I promised you. I do have a favor to ask."

"What is it, Ron?"

"My friend, her, Dick, would like to join us. He likes to watch."

"Ron, you promised just you and me!" exclaims Bobbie.

"Well, I have had too much to drink and I may need help in directing where to stick my cock."

"OK, just as long as you don't get it mixed up and I am penetrated by his cock!"

"Would it be so bad to get fucked twice tonight?" asks Ron.

"I need to take a shower. Meet me in the ballet room in fifteen minutes," says Bobbie.

"Ron, I am so confused. She is more than willing to be fucked by you, but last time she fought you. What has changed?" asks Richard.

"Persuasion, Dick! I do not think she wants the scene we had the last time I fucked her."

"Do you mean you raped her?"

"Well, not quite, Dick. We had a rough time and it took time for her to believe me when I told her the next encounter would be smoother."

"It sounds like a threat!"

"No, Dick, persuasion!"

HARD-ON FOR DEATH

B obbie takes a big risk and comes close to being raped again.

"Hey, honey, are you in here yet?" asks Ron when he and Richard enter the ballet room.

"Yes, Ron, I am here. I am ready for you," says Bobbie as she walks from the dark corner into Ron's view.

"Do you think I would skip out on you, Ron?"

"No, I guess not, but you are so willing," says Ron.

"Like I said, I had time to think about it and I knew I wouldn't be able to escape future encounters with you. I will even bend over the horse for you and my bare ass will be ready for your cock."

"Dick, I am feeling real tipsy right now. Take my hand and help me over to her."

"I must say I haven't seen such a perfect looking pussy," states Richard.

"Yeah, honey, your ass looks better tonight. Have you been toning it up?" asks Ron.

"No, Ron, you have had too much to drink. My ass is the same as it was the last time you fucked me, except no semen, yet. Are you going to get me to 'cum' this time?"

"I'll think about it, but first I am going to fuck you in case I pass out."

"Ron, you told her you would grant her request. Make her 'cum' like she asks," scolds Richard.

"Listen, Dick, I did not invite you here to harass me, and this bitch is just going to have to wait. Once I am finished with her, maybe you can make her 'cum'."

"Now, let me begin. Every time I look at your ass, bitch, I get a stiff hard on! Like I promised the last time, I will be gentle with you," says Ron.

"Ron, I am all wet. Hurry up."

"Oh, my God! Dick, help me with my zipper!"

"OK, bitch, I am ready!" Ron grasps his cock with his hand and stumbles to the vaulting horse.

"Ron, I can see your cock in the mirror. I want you to sink the whole length of it into my pussy, so remove your hand and place both hands behind your back. Yeah, that's it, now, thrust that shaft in!" orders Bobbie.

"OK, baby….wait, what the hell?" 'Swish'. "Oh, what the hell?…..Ah, the pain...my cock, it is gone! I am bleeding! You chopped off my cock. Who the hell are you?" moans Ron.

"It's me, Bobbie," she says as she emerges from the corner of the room.

"Who is that on the horse?" asks Ron.

"It was me! You raped me, remember, and now you will never be able to rape anyone again!"

"I am in so much pain and I am bleeding...my cock, where is it?"

"It's on the floor, you bastard."

"You can't just let me bleed to death."

"Yup, I can, and I will. You will suffer for what you did to me!"

"But, but, I was gentle with you……"

59

"Richard, put a gag in his mouth. I don't want to hear his pathetic pleads. Tie his hands and feet together," orders Bobbie.

"Ron, we are leaving. We will be back to retrieve your dead body. Too bad that you don't have a penis. You can't even relieve yourself from all of that pent-up semen!"

"Let's go, Richard. We will come back in a half hour," says Bobbie.

THE BOG

R ichard and Bobbie converse on what had just happened.

"Bobbie, you were correct in your planning you wouldn't get hurt," said Richard.

"Yes, do you believe I would bend over that horse and bare my ass to him again? No, miss blowup doll did it for me, and with him half crocked, he couldn't recognize a painted pussy from a real one. You did a good job, Richard, getting him drunk."

"I didn't know you were going to chop his penis off. What is that thing you used to cut it off?" Richard asks.

"It is a sword. I found a practice sword in the ballet room the night I was raped. I thought I would use it on him if I saw him again that night. Of course, I didn't see him. Being that it is a practice sword for fencing, I knew it didn't have an edge, so I went into the tool room one night, after my workout, and filed it down to a sharp edge."

"I didn't know you were so talented with tools."

"Richard, I am a very talented woman!"

"So, it was your plan to kill him, all along?"

"Yup, and my plan became a reality. I figured he should be made to suffer with the very act he forced upon me, except with a dummy blow-up doll. There was no way he was going to rape me again," says Bobbie.

"Suffer up to death?" asks Richard.

"Yes, so as soon as he was ready to penetrate miss blow-up doll, I would appear from the dark corner and swipe his penis off with the sword. I want him to suffer; I want him to bleed to death," says Bobbie.

"I was concerned you would have to bend over the horse."

"Richard, I wouldn't willingly expose my ass to just anyone; just you! Besides don't you know the difference between a real pussy and a painted one? You have seen mine enough..haven't you, Richard?"

"Bobbie, you are feeling better about yourself since the incident?" asks Richard.

"I am slowly getting there, and by the way, Richard, you put it on pretty thick back there in the gym saying, 'Wow, look at her ass!' didn't you?"

"Well, sweetheart, I was being truthful..very truthful!"

RICHARD AND BOBBIE RETURN TO THE BALLET ROOM AN HOUR LATER AND FIND RON DEAD ON THE FLOOR

"What is our next move, honey?" asks Richard.

"Richard, help me wrap him up in this garbage bag."

"What do you want me to do with his severed, penis?" asks Richard.

"Kick it in the bag. Seal off the bag and let's get him into the trunk of my car. Richard, please pull the car up to this door. I will clean up the blood on the floor. Luckily, most of it soaked into his trousers," says Bobbie.

"Where are we driving too, Bobbie?"

"We are going north to the town of Brantingham."

"It is at the edge of the Adirondacks, isn't it?" asks Richard.

"Yes, and then we go another two miles into the park where we travel the rest of the way on foot."

"Travel by foot; where are we going?" asks Richard.

———

"OK, Richard, we must be very careful out here. Let's cut these two saplings. We need to make a stretcher to drag this body to our destination."

"What or where is our destination, Bobbie?"

"About a mile from here is where we are going. Let's tie these two saplings together with the rope so there is about three feet of space between them. We can affix this branch, so it stabilizes the assembly."

"Bobbie, how is it you know all of this?"

"Sweetheart, as part of Officer Training, we learned first aid, rescue, and survival. Do you remember?"

"Yeah....ah, maybe not completely."

"Obviously, Richard, you were not concentrating while in the class. I suppose you had your mind elsewhere? Oh come on, you didn't even know me then, Richard!"

"I may not have known you then, but the anticipation was there."

"Just come on. We will take turns dragging this body to our destination," says Bobbie.

———

"Richard, we will need to carry the body the rest of the way," says Bobbie as they near a field of grass.

"Look at all the pretty grass here, right out in the middle of nowhere!" exclaims Richard.

"Honey, help me lift this bastard! You take his feet and I will take his head. Now let's slowly walk over there with him."

"Bobbie, this grass is so plush. It feels like my feet are floating."

"OK, here we are," says Bobbie as they lower the body to the grass.

"So, sweetheart, you were asking me why I have a saw with a long blade? I will show you," says Bobbie.

Bobbie thrusts the end of the saw blade down into the grass and pushes it all the way to the handle. "Now, I will cut an area of this grass," says Bobbie.

"What is this place, Bobbie? You are cutting into the soil like it is hot butter!"

"Help me move this grassy square I just cut out."

"Hey, I see water; what the hell!" says Richard.

"Help me push the body bag through this hole. Good, now we put the grassy square back," says Bobbie.

"I can't even see where you had cut it!" exclaims Richard.

"OK, Honey, I can now answer your questions. This area is a bog, a very big bog. It is an experiment in growing grasses in Coca-Cola®. We are standing on a huge lake of Coca-Cola® and the only thing between our feet and the Coke® is about two feet of soil, thus the spongy feel. We are standing on a floating garden," explains Bobbie.

"Holy, shit! I would have never guessed!" Richard exclaims.

"No one will ever find the body here, and with all the tannins in the Cola®, breakdown of the body tissues will be rather quick," says Bobbie.

"How did you know about this spot, sweetheart?"

"While at the gym, I overheard someone talking about it. I got maps and searched Google Earth® to find the location. I knew it was a great place to dispose of the body. Let's go back home, Richard, our job is done and a part of me is satisfied. Justice is served! Now I can start to work on building our relationship as it was before the rape," says Bobbie.

"Bobbie, sweetheart, will it be OK if I kiss you?"

"Oh, Richard, yes, please do!"

THEIR MOUTHS MEET AND WITH LIPS SLIGHTLY PARTED, THEIR TONGUES
DANCE AROUND EACH OTHER, JUST LIKE OLD TIMES. RICHARD FEELS A
STIFFNESS IN HIS GROIN WHILE BOBBIE FEELS A WELCOME WETNESS IN
HER PANTIES. SHE RELISHES THE FEELINGS OF AROUSAL COMING BACK
TO HER

"Richard, please remember we cannot tell Julia what we have done. We have to let things roll and the result will be an unsolved missing person."

"Are you going to tell Julia who tried to rape her that night?"

"Richard, I can't right away. We need to have some time elapse so as to not raise suspicion. It is unfortunate."

DOES SHE SUSPECT?

Back at the office, Bobbie engages in conversation with Julia.

"Good morning, Julia! What is in store for today?" asks Bobbie.

"To tell you the truth, Bobbie, it is pretty quiet around here. I like to feel that the community of Harford is safe today. Hopefully, it will stay that way. Now, it has been a little over a month and I have heard nothing of our missing pervert," states Julia.

"As you know, I have not received any further leads on him," says Bobbie.

"I should go over to the gym and interview the teenagers, again, and see if they learned any new information. You know they will not come forward to us, now, since divulging their sexual fantasies about him," states Julia.

"Julia, I need to tell you something that I should have told you, but I could not at the time."

"Bobbie, what is it? Is it about our missing person?"

"The time that I was raped, I couldn't get up enough energy to tell you who did it to me. I was concerned I would hurt you if I told you."

"Bobbie, I do not follow."

"Julia, the man who raped me is the missing person, Ron Linden."

"That pervert at the gym."

"Yes."

"How do you know it was him? You told me that you were blindfolded the entire time."

"I was blindfolded, but I recognized the cologne he was wearing. One night when I was leaving the gym, Ron held the door for me as I was approaching the exit. As I passed by, I noted his cologne. It was English Leather® cologne."

"As he brushed by me tying me to the vaulting horse, the night he raped me, I smelled the cologne."

"Another man could have been wearing the same cologne, so you can't be totally positive, can you?" asks Julia.

"Not from just that encounter, but what I have tell you next positively identifies him."

"You have my attention, Bobbie. What is it that you want to tell me?"

"Julia, while I was being raped, this man, Ron, compared my bare ass to another woman's."

"How disturbing!"

"Yeah, and he described the woman as……you!"

"What? I don't get it. How does he know what my bare ass looks like….wait a minute, Bobbie, are you telling me that Ron was the one who tried to rape me in the parking lot that night?"

"Yes, Julia, he even named you. I am sorry, Julia. I couldn't tell you. I did not want to hurt you and I knew my experiences were not concrete evidence in court to prosecute him."

"Bobbie, it is OK. I did suspect he was the one who attacked me after what we had witnessed during our workouts and my interview with the teenagers. I also knew I didn't have enough evidence to arrest him. It is a coincidence after attacking me and then raping you, he has gone missing. If I were to guess, someone he was involved with might just have caused his disappearance. What do you think, Bobbie?"

"Yeah, Julia, I suppose it could be so."

"Would you agree with me, Bobbie, we don't really want him found?"

"Yes, I would agree."

"Good riddance!" exclaims Julia.

"So, where do we go from here, Julia? Should we try to find out if he was involved with someone who might have caused his disappearance?"

"No, Bobbie, between you and I, the case is closed. No one will ever find him…."

"I agree Julia, it is over."

NICOLE TELLS ALL

Betsy, Julia's receptionist, is dialing into Julia's office.

"Yes, Betsy, what is it?" asks Julia.

"Chief, there is a young girl who just came in and would like to speak with you," Betsy replies.

"Please send her in."

"Well, hello. You are one of the girls from the gym. Let's see, I believe, Nicole?"

"Yes, ma'am, I am Nicole and we had a conversation about Ron's whereabouts. He is still missing, ya know."

"Yes, Nicole, we have found no further leads to his whereabouts. So, Nicole, what brings you here to my office? Do you have any leads involving his disappearance?"

"No, ma'am, I do not. I have come here, for another reason."

"OK, what is it, Nicole?"

"Mrs. Lillus, or should I call you Chief Lillus?"

"No, you can call me by my name, Julia."

"OK, Mrs. Lillus, I mean Julia, I am pregnant."

"OK Nicole, do you know who the father is?"

"Yes, it is Ron."

"You had told me you wanted to get 'laid' by him, so what is the issue? You knew, didn't you, the chance you would take in involving yourself in that way could lead to a pregnancy?"

"Well, no, not really because he always would wear condoms with us."

"With us?" asks Julia.

"Yes, I......er, we were not telling you the truth about us and Ron. Ron had sexual relations with us regularly."

"But, you explicitly expressed to me that you asked him to fuck you, as you put it?"

"Yes, it is true. I don't know about the other girls, but I asked for it because I felt the need to be wanted. I do not get much recognition from my family and I yearn for my father's affection. He does not pay attention to me and often tells me how ugly I am and I will never attract any men. Well, I am attractive to Ron and he always proves it."

"So, Ron provides recognition to you and makes you feel wanted and attractive, for which you so much lack from your father, by allowing him to have sex with you?" asks Julia.

"Yes."

"You say Ron always uses a condom when he has sexual relations with you?"

"Yes, he tells us that he has to be careful he doesn't get us pregnant because I am sixteen years old and some of the other girls are fourteen and fifteen."

"What happened? Did his condom break?"

"No Mrs. Lillus. One night while at the gym he was a little drunk. He came over to me after a while and told me that it was my time."

"Your time? For what?" Julia asks.

"It was time for him to fuck me. He had a way of picking us girls by way of specific times. I had told him I was not in the mood and I had my period. He grabbed my arm and ushered me to the ballet room where he told me it did not matter how I felt, he was going to fuck me because it was time. He said to me that he was looking forward to fucking me without a condom due to me having my period. I tried to tell him, but he put a gag on me."

"You tried to tell him what, Nicole?"

"I tried to tell him that I still wanted him to use a condom because I was not having my period. I used that excuse to try to get out of getting 'laid'. It was too late. He 'came' in me without a condom."

"He raped you, Nicole. You did not ask for it at the time?"

"No, I did not want him to fuck me that night. I think I just didn't want him near me."

"Maybe you were starting to see your actions were not getting you anywhere and he was using you?" asks Julia.

"Yes ma'am. What you had told me that night about my actions is correct. I know, now, the huge mistake I made and now I must suffer the consequences. I only want Ron to be found because I want him to support the expenses of his baby that I am carrying."

"Nicole, are you sure that Ron is the father?"

"Oh, yes, Ron stole my virginity and he has been the only one fucking me."

"What about the other girls? Do they know you are pregnant?"

"No, they don't."

"I think you should tell them, so they see the living proof of what the consequences can be with indiscriminate sexual activity. Nicole, I truly believe Ron will not be found," says Julia.

"Why do you say that?"

"It is just a feeling, but it doesn't matter. You need to concentrate on you and your baby."

"Mrs. Lillus, I mean Julia, I do not have any money and I am only sixteen! I am so scared!"

"What about your family, Nicole?"

"Oh, no, they will not help me, especially now that I am pregnant. They will think I was asking for it."

"Nicole, you were raped! It is all anyone needs to know. In that instance, you did not ask him to have sex with you. He violated you without consent. It is rape."

"Julia, will you help me? If my family doesn't accept me. What do I do? Where do I go?"

"Do you have time tonight to talk to your parents? I will go with you," suggests Julia.

"Yes, and thank you, ma'am," Nicole answers.

TOUGH LOVE

Nicole directs Julia to her home.

"Hello, Mrs. Peters. I am Chief Julia Lillus from the Harford Police Department. May I come in?" asks Julia.

"Nicole! Why are you here with a Police Officer? What trouble have you gotten yourself in?" asks Mrs. Peters.

"Mom please…." Nicole responds.

"Mrs. Peters, is your husband home?"

"Yes, he is in the living room watching the television."

"Is there a place we can talk?" asks Julia.

"Henry, can you come out here in the kitchen? We have the police here and Nicole is in trouble," yells Mrs. Peters.

"Ya, ya, ya…that kid is always in some kind of trouble," states Henry.

"Mr. Peters, I am Chief Julia Lillus from the Harford Police Department."

"Oh, yeah, you are the new Police Chief. Quite a pretty one too," remarks Mr. Peters.

"Mr. and Mrs. Peters, Nicole asked me to come here with her as support and she is not in trouble," says Julia.

"Why are you crying, Nicole," asks Mrs. Peters.

"Mom and dad, I have something to tell you which you may not like to hear, but it is even harder for me to explain. I was raped, and I am pregnant!" cries Nicole.

"What the hell, Nicole! You go and spread your legs to a man and then come running to us for our support!" exclaims Mr. Peters.

"Mr. Peters! Nicole was raped! She did not ask for this. She is asking for your understanding," Julia states.

"Nicole, you should have least asked him to wear a condom," says Mrs. Peters.

"Mr. and Mrs. Peters, do I have to educate you on what rape is?" Julia asks angrily.

"No, we know, but Nicole shouldn't have allowed a situation like that to happen. Usually rape comes from being in the 'wrong crowd'," says Mr. Peters.

"Look, you two, Nicole needs your support. She did not ask for this nor is it a result of being in with the 'wrong crowd'. I will not sit here listening to you belittling her with your un-called-for remarks. Nicole is with child and you need to think about her and her baby's well-being, nothing more! Are you going to be supportive of her?" asks Julia.

"Well, we will try," says Mrs. Peters.

"Nicole will need rape counseling and a plan set up for nurturing the baby while she is carrying it and care for after he or she is born. Are you willing to do this for your daughter, Mr. and Mrs. Peters?" asks Julia.

"We don't have much money. How can we do this?" asks Mrs. Peters.

"Don't worry about the money at this point. I am looking only for your willingness to support Nicole," says Julia.

"I am done, here. I am not in favor of supporting a bastard child!" exclaims Mr. Peters.

"Mrs. Peters, is this your feeling as well?" asks Julia.

"Well, I do not know. I would like to help, but Henry, well he is not willing. I can't do it myself. Isn't there a shelter for girls such as Nicole?" asks Mrs. Peters.

"Nicole, please go pack up your things you want and need. I will wait here for you and I will take you to my home," says Julia.

"Are you taking Nicole with you?" asks Mrs. Peters.

"Yes, and she can stay with me until she is ready to come back, here, to her home and you two are receptive to supporting her," answers Julia.

"Good luck with her, Chief. You will find she is trouble, you will see!" exclaims Mr. Peters.

"What I am going to say to you two is off the record and I am speaking this not as a Police Officer, but a normal caring human being. You are both pathetic!" Julia exclaims.

"Julia, I am all set. Can we go now?" asks Nicole.

"Yes, honey, let's go."

"Julia, I cannot thank you enough! I was so wrong, and I am so sorry to put you through all of this. My parents reacted the way I expected. I guess I just am not the right daughter for them."

"Nicole, don't dwell in the past. We all make mistakes. Your parents may come around given time, but for now, you are with me and you and I will have a great time preparing you for your baby," Julia responds.

"Julia, maybe sometime you can tell me what real love is and how it feels."

"That I can do, Nicole."

"Here we are, home sweet home. It is an apartment, but I will be sure to make it comfortable for you," says Julia.

"Julia, would it be all right if I gave you a hug? I am so grateful for you and what you are doing for me."

"Sure honey, this is a part of feeling love," Julia responds.

WHILE NICOLE IS SETTLING IN, JULIA PLACES A CALL TO BOBBIE

"Bobbie, do you remember the teenage girl we see at the gym?"

"Which one?"

"The olive-skinned girl with the long reddish brown hair. She is quite attractive. Her name is Nicole."

"Yeah, I know the one."

"She is pregnant with Ron's baby."

"What? She finally got her wish to get fucked?"

"Well, not exactly. She was raped by him."

"Oh, hell, has that bastard fucked every woman in Harford?"

"Her family has disowned her, and she is staying with me."

"Oh, Julia, you have such a heart of gold!" exclaims Bobbie.

"I feel that this is a turning point in her life. She no longer wants to be permissive and with my help, she will no longer need a man's sexual acts to prove she is loved. I will help her with self-esteem. She will make a great mother," Julia says.

"If you need any help, Julia, I am just a phone call away," says Bobbie.

BABY TIME

R ichard gives Bobbie what she is asking for.

―――――――――

"Richard, how is your dinner?" asks Bobbie.

"It is exquisite like always."

"Honey, you look a little tired tonight. Is there anything I can do for you," asks Bobbie.

"Sweetheart, you do so much for me. There is nothing else left."

"Come over here, Richard. Put your arms around me. Do you remember the 'hot sex' we had when we were first married?"

"Yes, I certainly do!" exclaims Richard.

"Would it be OK, if I requested a review?"

"You mean a review of what we used to do?"

"Yes, but I want it to be better," Bobbie says with enthusiasm.

Bobbie reaches down and presses her hand against Richard's groin. The response is immediate, and Bobbie feels his hardness.

"Bobbie, sweetheart, you are sure you are ready for this?"

"Honey, I have always wanted this, but couldn't bear to let my feelings out after the rape. I love you so much! Yes, I am ready. Please do what you wish with me," says Bobbie.

Richard picks up Bobbie in his arms and carries her across the threshold of their bedroom doorway. He gently places her on their bed. He places his hands on her sides and slowly slides up to her arms, lifting them over her head. Gently he slips her blouse up over her head exposing her breasts enclosed in her bra. As he unhooks the clasp, between the cups of her bra, he sees, once again, her breasts he has visualized in his mind for the lack of having access to them since the rape. Her nipples are erect, and he bends down to suckle them.

"Oh, Richard, how I have missed this! I think I want to have a baby."

"Anything you say Bobbie, anything you say," says Richard as he proceeds to lift her skirt and remove her rose-colored panties.

BUILDING A RELATIONSHIP

J ulia and Nicole have a heart-to-heart conversation.

"Nicole, let's go out and get you some new clothes to wear. You are starting to show and I will bet your clothes are starting to become uncomfortable," says Julia.

"OK, thanks," says Nicole.

"Julia, can I ask you a question?"

"Sure, Nichol, ask me anything you want."

"Were you married?"

"Yes, Nichol, I used to be married to a wonderful man."

"Where is he? What happened?"

"It is a long story, Nichol, but he was a sick man and he isn't here anymore."

"How did it feel to have a man around who wasn't just after sex?"

"Nicole, my husband, Tim, and I had such a wonderful relationship. We loved each other immensely. We complimented each other. What one of us didn't have, the other would give. We did things together and we were willing to give our full attention to our marriage and relationship, so it could flourish as time went by."

"Was your husband true to you? Did he need to gawk at other women to be happy?"

"No, Tim didn't need any of that because I gave him what he needed."

"Did you give him sex? I mean, what is the act of sex like, being married?"

"Speaking of relationships, a man and woman take vows when married to be true to each other and willing to give each other what is needed to formulate the 'glue' which keeps the relationship flourishing. Tim and I enjoyed enriching sex interludes, an essential part of our marriage relationship. Sex within a marriage relationship is the communal give and take of one's self. It is the fulfillment of mutual desire. Each partner gives to the other the ultimate experience of sharing the most intimate part of their being. It is pure pleasure and the willingness to explore each other's bodies."

"So, it is not forced? It is to be a mutual thing between each partner?" asks Nicole.

"Yes, it is mutual and there is no room for forcing one person onto another. It is far from what you have experienced. It is a commitment and not a one-night stand. The feeling is of oneness with your partner and shuts out all other influences. Someday, you will experience this when you have a husband."

"Do you think I will have a husband, Julia, after what I have done?"

"Honey, you will have a husband if it is to be. You will then, feel a kind of love like which Tim and I shared."

SHE IS IN THE FREEZER

Betsy receives a call and informs Julia she is wanted on the line.

"Chief, I just received a call from a home on the West Side. The children were playing in the basement and found a woman in the chest freezer while looking for ice cream," says Betsy.

"Did you get any specifics?" asks Julia.

"No, they just said to hurry and get over there," replies Betsy.

"Richard and Bobbie, would you please come into my office? We have another possible homicide on the West Side," states Julia.

"Bobbie, what is the address, again?" asks Richard.

"225 Harbison," replies Bobbie.

"I am Officer Peltz and this is my partner Officer Fritz. We understand you have a body in a freezer in the basement?"

"Yes, yes, my nephews found her while looking for some ice cream. Those kids are traumatized."

"Why are they traumatized?" asks Officer Fritz.

"She has no clothes on and she is all bloodied up. Those boys have never seen a woman with her clothes off! They have questions."

"Please lead us to the basement, ma'am," says Officer Peltz.

"You boys have seen enough, now go upstairs," says Officer Fritz.

"She looks pretty chopped up," says Officer Fritz.

"Fritz, call Forensics and get them down here. We need DNA testing and a Medical Examiner to tell us what the hell we see," orders Officer Peltz.

"What's your first impression, doc?" asks Officer Peltz.

"An autopsy will need to be done to be sure of the time and method of death, but my impression is that she looks about twenty years of age, slim build and highly bruised between her thighs. I would say she has been penetrated under force. The knife lacerations, at first glance, appear to be twenty in number. Her skull shows signs of a blunt object used to dislodge her teeth. One last thing; someone has messed her up pretty badly down there."

"Oh, shit, who or why would someone do that?" asks Officer Peltz.

"Get the Coroner down here to take the body," says Officer Fritz to the Medical Examiner.

WHO IS SHE?

Officer Bobbie Fritz starts to question about the body.

"Hello, we have already met and whom are we talking to?"

"My name is Ethel Fulmer."

"Ma'am, we have a few questions for you. Do you know this girl found in your freezer?" asks Officer Fritz.

"No, I have never seen her before. I do not know who she is."

"Ma'am, where is your husband?"

"He is at work. He works the late shift over at the foundry."

"When do you expect him to be home?"

"He comes home at around six in the morning."

"What time did he come home this morning?"

"I suppose at six. I do not know, I was sleeping. I did not see him until about seven and then he went to bed."

"When did he leave for work today?"

"He left at nine pm like he always does."

"I have just a couple more questions. Do you know if your husband has any lady friends and do you have reason to believe that he might be seeing other women?" asks Officer Fritz.

"I don't think so other than maybe some he works with. My husband is a loyal man and he loves me. He would not be seeing other women."

"Oh, and do you have a daughter?" asks Officer Peltz.

"Yes."

"How old is she?"

"She is fourteen."

"Where is she now?"

"She is at her girlfriend's house. She spent the night over there."

"Thank you, ma'am, it is all the questions we have at the moment," says Officer Fritz.

———————

"Richard, we need to interview the husband. Can you get over here tomorrow at seven am to interview," asks Bobbie.

"Sure, let me tell her I will be coming to question her husband," says Richard.

———————

"Julia, we don't have much to go on except the body is a young female at the age of around twenty; stabbed numerous times; had been hit in the face with a blunt object and possibly raped. She is pretty messed up... her lady parts. I think she was butchered down there," says Richard.

"What? That is the most grossest thing that I have heard of since becoming Chief," states Julia.

"I am going to interview the husband tomorrow morning. He works the overnight shift at the foundry. Hopefully we will get some information from the Coroner soon, once he finishes the autopsy," says Richard.

FRED FULMER

T he following morning, Richard makes his way to 225 Harbison
to interview the husband.

"Hello. Are you Mr. Fulmer?" asks Richard.

"Yes, I am Fred Fulmer. My wife, Ethel, said you would be here.
What do you want to know?"

"By the way, my name is Deputy Officer Peltz from the Harford
Police Department. You are aware a body of a young female was
found in your chest freezer in the basement?"

"Yeah, my wife told me about it."

"So, you didn't know anything about it until your wife told you?"

"That is correct!"

"Oh, Hi, honey, how was your night over at Jeans?" asks Fred.

"It was fine, daddy," answers Vicky.

"Well, who is this young lady?" asks Officer Peltz.

"This is my sweet daughter Vicky Lynn. She had an overnight at
her friend's house last night," says Fred.

"Nice to meet you Ms. Vicky," says Officer Peltz.

"We have some business to tend too, so why don't you go and see if your mother needs any help," suggests Fred.

"Oh, daddy, must I? I want to be with you today!" exclaims Vicky Lynn.

"That's OK, honey, now run along," says Fred as he gives her a slap on her buttocks as she leaves.

"How old is your daughter, Mr. Fulmer?"

"She is fourteen."

"She seems to be such a mature young lady," says Officer Peltz.

"She is a sweetheart, that girl, she is a sweetheart."

"Mr. Fulmer, what kind of work do you do?"

"I currently work at the foundry. I am a smelter."

"Oh, wow, it sure is a hot job working around all that molten steel," says Officer Peltz.

"Yes, it is."

"How many employees does the foundry have?"

"We have about twenty of us who work in the in the factory and about another twenty or so in administration, and most of them are female."

"Oh, so you don't have any females who work in the factory?"

"Just a couple of females."

"I see," says Officer Peltz

"Yeah, but they can hold their own! You don't want to cross them!" exclaims Fred.

"Mr. Fulmer, I understand you work the overnight shift?"

"Yup, and I will need to go to bed shortly in order to get up to work tonight."

"Mr. Fulmer, how do you think that woman got into your chest freezer?"

"I don't have a clue."

"Did you see her, Mr. Fulmer?"

"No, I was at work, but my wife told me about her. She was pretty messed up wasn't she?"

"Yes, Mr. Fulmer, she was," says Officer Peltz.

"She was a young one?"

"Yes, Mr.Fulmer, I would venture to guess she was a college girl attending the nearby college. What is the name?" asks Officer Peltz.

"Roosevelt," says Fred.

"That's correct."

"Mr. Fulmer, I am just wondering, how far is the college from the foundry?"

"I would say about a mile. Why do you ask?"

"Just wondering, that is all," says Officer Peltz.

"Vicky Lynn, you not going to help your momma?" asks Fred.

"Yes, Daddy, I did, but I want to know when you will be finished. I want to see you before you go to work."

"I have to go to bed soon, but I will be sure to see you, sweetheart. Now run along," says Fred, once again giving her a slap on her buttocks and hesitates with a stare as her skirt rises exposing her bare cheeks.

"Mr. Fulmer, it appears that Vicky Lynn is the apple of your eyes," says Officer Peltz.

"Yes, I don't know what I would do without her."

"Well, Mr. Fulmer, I don't have any more questions at the moment. I will be in touch if I think of anything else," says Officer Peltz.

ONE YEAR AGO

E thel notices a change in her husband Fred.

"Fred dear, are you trying to get me pregnant, again?" asks Ethel.

"No, not really, I believe we have enough on our hands with thirteen-year-old Vicky Lynn," answers Fred.

"You have stepped up your game and now we are having sex almost every day," remarks Ethel.

"Oh, but you love it, honey," says Fred.

"I am kind of getting sore down there. Maybe we should slow down some?" asks Ethel.

"Slow down, Ethel? I am at the prime of my life and my zest for sex is increasing as each day progresses," says Fred.

"Fred, you must find other ways to diminish your sex drive, or at least satisfy it. Maybe you should start masturbating more often," says Ethel.

"My hand is no match for your pussy, Ethel. I suggest you find a way to toughen that pussy of yours. I won't stop fucking you and as many times I desire!" exclaims Fred.

"Fred, I don't know what has come over you! I might need to be away from home more often. Get yourself a blow-up doll, Fred! You can fuck it as much as you want!" says Ethel angrily.

"You can't escape me, Ethel! I will have my way with you anytime I want! You will have to be home sometime. Vicky Lynn needs her momma!" exclaims Fred.

THE STRIP CLUB

F red goes to the strip club earlier than usual during the week.

"Hey Fred! What are you doing here on a Wednesday night? I thought your night was Fridays. Isn't it when your Diva Debbie does the lap dance for you?" asks Larry.

"Look, Larry, I needed to get a hard on. Ethel is holding back on letting me fuck her."

"Well, this place will do it for you. At about eight pm, Darcie is doing her pole dance and I understand that she has an open crotch in her shorts. The guys tell me if she is offered enough money, she will come over to you and show you her snatch as she collects your money," says Larry.

"That is exactly what I need right now. I haven't had any pussy for some time and I am ready to explode!" says Fred.

"I don't know if Darcie does lap dances, but you could always ask," says Larry.

"Oh, my God, Larry, Darcie is gorgeous, and look at that ass! I would fuck her in an instance!" exclaims Fred.

"You got enough money to give her, so she will show you her snatch?" asks Larry.

"I have plenty of money, Larry."

"Hey, honey! I like your moves. I have a little present for you. Why don't you come over her and I will give it to you," says Fred.

Darcie slips off the pole she has been dancing on and provocatively walks over to the edge of the stage. As Fred is reaching out his hand full of bills, Darcie bends over and collects them. As she stands up, Larry gestures to Fred.

"Fred, give her more money!" exclaims Larry.

Fred pulls more bills out of his pocket and stretches his hand out to Darcie. This time, Darcie walks over to the edge of the stage and squats down directly in front of him and as she his collecting the bills from his hand, spreads her knees apart.

"Oh, Jesus! Larry, her crotch in her shorts is open just like you said. Oh my God, I saw that beautiful snatch. There are jewels on it and oh, so pink it is! I think I am going to 'cum' right here in my pants!" exclaims Fred.

"Fred, turn around, Darcie has a note to pass to you," says Larry.

"Thank you, sweetheart and you have a lovely pussy, I may add," Fred says to Darcy as she starts to walk back to the pole to continue her dance.

"Fred, what does the note say? Come on, hurry, open it."

"Larry, she is inviting me for a private lap dance with her for one hundred dollars."

"Do you have it, Fred?" asks Larry.

"I sure do and I am going to fuck her for that amount."

"Fred, I don't think any of these girls will fuck you. They only go so far, at least that is what other guys say."

"Well, Larry, this guy is going to fuck Miss Darcie," says Fred.

A little later, Fred goes into the private viewing area of the strip club. He sees the door with the sign reading 'Darcie's Lair'. He steps up to the door and knocks.

"Come in!" says the voice on the other side of the door.

"So, you like my pussy?" asks Darcie.

"Yes, I do. It gives me a hard on," says Fred.

"Do you have my money?"

"I sure do!" Fred exclaims.

"Well, for fifty more dollars I will give you a blow job and then we can see what happens next," says Darcie.

"Will fifty dollars more buy my way to fuck you?" asks Fred.

"Just a blow job," Darcie responds.

"Here, here, fifty more dollars," says Fred.

"OK, buddy, unzip those pants and get your dick out. I see it is already stiff, so let's get on with it," says Darcie.

As she bends down to his groin, Fred notices she hasn't changed her outfit. She still has the crotchless shorts on. Fred thinks, "Maybe she will allow me to fuck her."

Darcie places her lips around Fred's cock and starts to engulf it in her mouth. With an up and down motion along his shaft, she starts to suck.

"Oh, God, honey, it is just ecstasy!" exclaims Fred.

"I won't let you 'cum' in my mouth, so I won't be on it very long," explains Darcie.

Suddenly, Darcie stops caressing Fred's cock with her mouth. She turns her back to Fred as she stands and moves toward him to straddle his legs as he is sitting in the chair. Fred's cock is still aroused and erect as he places his hands on Darcie's hips and slowly pulls her down onto his lap, while lining up his cock with her pussy. He pulls her down as her pussy engulfs it. She immediately starts to shift her ass in an up and down motion, stroking his cock.

"Sweet ecstasy, honey! Keep it up! I am in heaven! Oh...oh..oh, I am going to 'cum'! Here it comes!" exclaims Fred.

Immediately Darcie hops up off his cock just as his load blasts into the air.

"Honey, you took the joy out of it!" exclaims Fred.

"Your money does not buy me accepting your 'diz' in my mouth or my pussy," says Darcie.

———

"Fred, what took you so long?" asks Larry.

"I fucked her!"

"What Fred? You didn't!"

"Larry, I fucked her!"

———

FRED CONFRONTS ETHEL ABOUT HAVING SEX

———

"Ethel, we need to fuck! I need to fuck!" exclaims Fred.

"Fred, I can't. You have me worn out! I don't know what has gotten into you, but suddenly wanting sex as much as you are asking for it, is not like you. We went through this a year ago and whatever you did worked. You have reverted back?" asks Ethel.

"Well, a man has got to do what a man has got to do!" exclaims Fred.

"Fred, Vicky Lynn is home. We can't have sex when she is home. You know she hears everything," says Ethel.

"Let's invite her in. At the age of fourteen, she needs to learn about sex sooner or later," says Fred.

"Fred Fulmer! What has gotten into you? You are disgusting! Are you watching porn movies while at work, or something?" asks Ethel.

"Come on baby, it is just a joke. Now follow me into the bedroom, lie down, and spread those legs wide," says Fred.

"I will not, Fred, and as a matter of fact, I am not sure when I will be ready to have sex with you, if ever! I refuse to be treated as if I am a whore. I am your wife!" exclaims Ethel.

A FEW WEEKS AFTER FRED'S FIRST VISIT TO THE STRIP CLUB AND HIS ENCOUNTER WITH MISS DARCIE, FRED IS FEELING SEXUAL ANXIETY DUE TO ETHEL REFUSING TO HAVE SEX WITH HIM

"Fred, you going to see Darcie tonight at the strip club?" asks Larry.

"I don't know, Larry. It is getting quite expensive."

"Do you need to see her snatch every time we are here? Do you need to fuck her as well?" asks Larry.

"I do. Ethel is refusing to fuck me. She is mad at me because of a remark I made to her and says I am wearing her out," says Fred.

"Fred, you do know going to those strip clubs makes you hornier, don't you?" asks Larry.

"Yeah, I do, but I really need sex, a lot of sex to survive!" exclaims Fred.

"What are you going to do, Fred?"

"Tonight, will have to be the last night, at least for a while, Larry."

"What or how are you going to 'survive' as you say, without Ethel getting you 'laid'?"

"I have a plan, Larry. I have a plan."

FRED RETURNS TO HIS HOME AND SUMMONS VICKY LYNN

"Vicky Lynn! Vicky Lynn! Are you home?"

"Yes, I am daddy!"

"Where is momma?"

"She went to the library. She said she would be back in a couple of hours."

"Come over here sweetheart. I have something to tell you," says Fred.

VICKY LYNN

A couple of weeks pass by and Vicky Lynn is awakening from a nightmarish sleep.

"Vicky Lynn! Vicky Lynn!"

"What daddy?"

"Honey, you know you are my special girl, don't you?"

"Yes, daddy, I do."

"Where is momma?" asks Fred.

"She went to the grocery store. I wanted to go with her," says Vicky Lynn.

"Sweetheart, you do know we need to be alone, don't you?"

"Oh daddy do we have to?"

"Honey, I told you, special girls deserve special treatments."

"But, daddy, I am sore down there because you do it to me just about every day."

"I told you it will get better. The more it is used the less it will be soar. Come, now, Vicky Lynn, what are those tears for?"

"Oh, daddy…."

"Sweetheart, come on over here. Now, lie down on the bed."

THE SURVEILLANCE

Richard has been thinking about his questioning of Fred Fulmer a few weeks past. He is bothered and must talk to Julia and Bobbie.

"Chief Lillus…"

"Richard, and this goes for you too, Bobbie, call me Julia. You do not have to be so formal."

"OK, Julia, I am concerned with the questioning I had with Mr. Fulmer a few weeks back. Something is strange about that man and it might shed some light on the murder case of that young woman," says Richard.

"What do you mean, Richard?" asks Julia.

"Well, the Fulmer's have a fourteen-year-old daughter named Vicky Lynn. I met her while I was questioning Mr. Fulmer and noted that he has a different kind of relationship with her; different from a normal father daughter relationship."

"What are you getting at, Richard?" asks Bobbie.

"Vicky Lynn talks to her father like a five-year-old might. When

Fulmer told her to run along and help her momma, he patted her on the buttocks and stared at her when her skirt flew up. He was definitely staring at her bare cheeks."

"If I were to take a guess, Mr. Fulmer is having sexual relations with his daughter," says Julia.

"We need to stop that!" exclaims Bobbie.

"We can't right now. We need further proof and at the same time I think that this may lead us to more information to what happened to that poor young lady found in their chest freezer," says Julia.

"I think we need to set up surveillance on Mr. Fulmer," says Bobbie.

"I agree, Bobbie. Go ahead. You and Richard set it up," says Julia.

"Richard, in your conversation with Mr. Fulmer, did he mention he was a butcher for the IGA before he got the job at the foundry?" asks Julia.

"No, he didn't," answers Richard.

"I did some investigating on Mr. Fulmer and found he was a butcher by trade," says Julia.

"That young lady was pretty cut up. I wonder if there is a connection?" ponders Bobbie.

"Could be," says Julia.

"Richard, I think we should go over to the college tonight and watch for a while," says Bobbie.

"I thought we are watching Mr. Fulmer," says Richard.

"Just watch. I have a hunch we will be seeing Mr. Fulmer," says Bobbie.

THAT EVENING, BOBBIE AND RICHARD TRAVEL OVER TO THE COLLEGE DORMITORIES

"What time is it, Richard?" asks Bobbie.

"It is about 9:30. Nothing seems to be going on at the college tonight," says Richard.

"OK, you might be correct, Richard. Let's get on over to the foundry," says Bobbie.

"Wait a minute, Bobbie! A car is coming into the dormitory parking lot. The college curfew is in effect at this time of night, so I wonder what this is all about," says Richard.

"Do you recognize the person getting out of the car, Richard?"

"I don't...wait a minute, it looks like the person is Mr. Fulmer."

"Look, Richard, a female is coming out of the dormitory and is walking toward him."

"It appears she knows him by the way they are embracing and kissing. Wow, he doesn't waste any time. I wonder if he plans to strip all the clothes off her right in front of us," says Richard.

"We just have to wait and see what happens. It looks as if he is going to fuck her in the car," says Bobbie.

"Let's wait it out, Bobbie," says Richard.

"Just as we thought. They leave nothing to the imagination with leaving the car door open. He is definitely fucking her," says Bobbie.

"We now know Fulmer is fucking more than just his daughter," says Bobbie.

"Yeah, but I see no connections to the murder of the woman. Maybe he is just a pervert and not our murderer," says Richard.

NEWS FROM THE CORONER

S am has finished with the initial autopsy of the murdered female.

"Chief Lillus, Sam here."

"Yes, Sam, what do you have for me?" asks Julia.

"The murder victim is a young female about twenty years of age. She had been stabbed numerous times, but whoever did this butchered her genitals. Without going into much detail, all I can say is that, outside of her vagina, there aren't any recognizable parts left."

"I am to assume there was penetration before the butchering?" asks Julia.

"Yes, there are signs of penetration and certainly under protest by the looks of the bruises on her inner thighs," says Sam.

"All of this doesn't make much sense. An assault, rape, butchering, and then stashed into a chest freezer," says Julia.

"I will be sure to contact you if I find anything further to help solve the case," says Sam.

"Thanks, Sam."

REBELLION

E thel notices that Vicky Lynn is acting quite peculiar.

"Fred, what is the matter with Vicky Lynn?"

"I don't know, Ethel. I did not know anything was wrong with her."

"I have noticed tears running down her cheeks when she is alone. She is very quiet lately; it is not like her," says Ethel.

"Maybe she is sick and doesn't feel well. I am sure that is all."

"Fred, I think it is more than that. While making her bed this morning, I noticed a bit of blood on her sheets."

"Oh, Ethel, she is of age to have her period, you know."

"Fred, I know what that discharge looks like, and it isn't it. I am going to take her to the doctor and have her checked out," says Ethel.

"Wait just a minute, Ethel. I think you are over reacting. We should wait a few days to see if she improves. I don't want to spend money on a doctor just for a virus," says Fred.

"Well, OK, I don't like it," says Ethel.

"Vicky Lynn, come in here! I want to speak to you!"

"Yes, daddy, what do you want to speak to me about?"

"You have disappointed me. You have been sloppy. Blood on your sheets?"

"Daddy, I told you I was hurt down there. It is not toughening up like you said. You hurt me every time you stick it into me. I am worried I will get pregnant? I can't take it any longer," says Vicky Lynn.

"You will take it! I will just take you somewhere that momma can't see…."

"Momma knows?"

"No, momma doesn't know, but she has seen the blood on your bed sheets, your tears, and experienced your quietness," says Fred.

"Daddy, I beg of you, please no more!"

"Special girls get special treatments," says Fred.

"No, daddy, I am not your special girl! I am not your whore!"

"Vicky Lynn, I don't want to hear that sort of language from you!"

"Why not, daddy? Do you think I am so naive that I don't know what you are doing to me? You do that to me for your own pleasure; certainly not mine!" exclaims Vicky Lynn.

"Young lady, you will comply with my wishes, and right now, while momma isn't here, you will lie down and let me in," orders Fred.

"No, daddy, no! You are hurting me! Please don't tie my hands!"

"Listen, honey, it will be much easier if you just spread your legs."

"No! No! I won't do it!"

"I will do it for you, now relax!"

"Oh, daddy, you are hurting me," cries Vicky Lynn.

ETHEL FULMER

At the Harford Police Department, a frantic woman hurriedly comes through the door.

"Yes, Betsy, what is it?" asks Julia.

"Chief, there is a woman out here who insists on talking to you."

"Thank you, Betsy, send her in."

"Chief Lillus?"

"Yes, what can I do for you?"

"Chief, my name is Ethel Fulmer, Fred Fulmer's wife."

"Oh, yes, you are the family with the young lady found in your chest freezer?"

"Yes, but I am here because of another matter. You see, I brought this bed sheet and want to know if you can tell me something about it?"

"I don't follow, Mrs. Fulmer."

"It is about my daughter Vicky Lynn...I...I think my husband Fred is having sex with her."

"How do you know this and do you have proof? Did your daughter, Vicky Lynn, tell you this?"

"No, but I have her bed sheet, here, and it has blood stains on it."

"Mrs. Fulmer, how do you know that the stain isn't from your daughter's mensural period? I am assuming she is having periods?"

"Yes, she started them when she was twelve. This stain does not look like a typical stain from a mensural period."

"Mrs. Fulmer, what is it you want me to do?"

"I want you to do additional tests and see if there is other evidence."

"So, you want me to test whether there is any of your husband's semen on the bed sheet?"

"Something like that," says Mrs. Fulmer.

"We don't do that, Mrs. Fulmer, but you can do the test yourself."

"Oh, how so?"

"Get yourself a black light from a tropical fish store and move it above the bed sheet. You will see semen stains, if there are any, but the test is still not evidence enough to prove he is having sexual relations with your daughter. It would take DNA testing, Mrs. Fulmer, why don't you try to get your daughter to confess to this?"

"I will try," says Mrs. Fulmer.

"Chief, I am starting to get the feeling that my husband is somehow tied to that murdered girl."

"Why do you say that, Mrs. Fulmer? Do you have new information for me?" asks Julia.

"No, it is just a feeling."

VICKY LYNN IS MISSING

E thel notices that Vicky Lynn isn't in her bedroom.

"Fred, where is Vicky Lynn?" asks Ethel.

"I don't know. She hasn't come home from school yet," says Fred.

"School is over by now, and it isn't like her to not come straight home," says Ethel.

"You worry too much, Ethel, I am sure she will show up soon."

"Was she acting OK when you saw her this morning?" asks Ethel.

"Oh, yeah, she was back as her typical self. Talking up a storm," says Fred.

BETSY RECEIVES A PHONE CALL FROM A FRANTIC WOMAN

"Chief, I just received a call from a frantic Mrs. Fulmer, reporting her daughter is missing. She said she was on her way over to see you," says Betsy, the receptionist.

"Ok, send her in when she arrives," says Julia.

"Hello, again, Mrs. Fulmer. What is going on with your daughter, Vicky Lynn?" asks Julia.

"My daughter went off to school this morning and has not come home. She always comes home promptly."

"Are you sure she didn't stop at a friend's house?"

"No, she would never do that without telling us. I am afraid something bad has happened to her," says Mrs., Fulmer.

"I think you should give her a little more time to show up at home. We do not issue missing persons reports until after a person has been missing over twenty-four hours," says Julia.

WHILE AT THE POLICE DEPARTMENT, ETHEL FULMER TALKS TO JULIA ABOUT THE WHAT SHE FOUND ON VICKY LYNN'S BED SHEET

"Chief, I got the black light like you told me and when I turned it on over Vicky Lynn's bed sheet, I saw semen stains."

"You can't prove they are semen stains and if they are, whose are they? Are you sure your daughter isn't seeing a boy? Maybe it isn't your husband," says Julia.

"Vicky Lynn is a sweet girl and I know that she isn't sexually active. I have had many discussions with her on sex and boys."

"Yeah, but you never know about teenagers. We will start looking for her and see if we can find some leads to where she might be," says Julia.

"Oh thank you, Chief."

ANOTHER MURDER

R ichard and Bobbie are eager to report to Julia their findings
with the surveillance of Fred Fulmer.

"Richard, how are you and Bobbie doing with your surveillance of
Mr. Fulmer?" asks Julia.

"He goes to the college like clockwork and the same thing
happens; girl meets him; he fucks her in the backseat of his car with
the door open," says Richard.

"Are you able to recognize whether it is the same girl?" asks Julia.

"Sometimes it is the same girl. The only common thing is that all
the girls are college girls who attend the Roosevelt College," says
Richard.

"We need a DNA test done with a sample of Mr. Fulmer's semen,"
says Julia.

"Bobbie, what do you say we stop the surveillance after tonight,"
says Richard.

"I have to agree. We have a pattern, but it does not help us with the case. All we have determined is Mr. Fulmer makes his rounds fucking college girls," says Bobbie.

DURING BOBBIE AND RICHARD'S LAST SURVEILLANCE OF MR. FULMER, THEY SEE SOMETHING THEY HAVEN'T SEEN IN THE OTHER SURVEILLANCES

"Hey, Bobbie, will you look at that. This is the first time one of those college girls actually turns down Mr. Fulmer," says Richard.

"Yeah, it looks as if she isn't buying his advances. Whoa, did you see that? He slapped her across the face and she kicked him in the groin. Well, I guess that ended it. He didn't get any pussy from her," says Bobbie.

JULIA CALLS RICHARD AND BOBBIE INTO HER OFFICE

"Hey guys, we have another missing person. This time it is a girl from the Roosevelt College Dormitory," says Julia.

"The Fulmer girl still missing?" asks Richard.

"Yes, and I just got word that our murder victim's parents have come forward to claim their daughter. They were abroad and did not know she was missing from the college," says Julia.

"I am starting to see a pattern, here," says Bobbie.

"Yeah, we have three females missing; one is our college murder victim; one is a missing college girl; and the other is Vicky Lynn. The only pattern is that they are all very young," says Richard.

"Chief Lillus?"

"Yes, this is Chief Julia Lillus. What can I do for you?"

"We have a dead body down here at the college. It is a female and the poor girl, well, she has been cut up pretty badly."

"I am on my way," says Julia.

"Hello, Chief Lillus, my name is Tom. I am the dorm security guard. Follow me. I will take you to the body. She is in the dumpster over there. I hope you are not squeamish because she is in real bad shape."

"Betsy, can I speak with Richard or Bobbie?" asks Julia.

"Richard is the only one in the office, so I will put you through to him."

"Thanks, Betsy."

"Richard, the body over here at the college dormitory, is very similar to our murder victim found in the chest freezer. She appears to be in her early twenties; quite bruised; stabbed numerous times; and disfigured in her genitals. The dorm security guard recognizes her as a college girl from his dormitory," says Julia.

"Richard, please give Sam a call to get him down here to pick up the body," says Julia.

SAM

S am finishes his autopsy on the second female murder victim.

"Hello, Sam?"

"Yes, this is Sam. Is this Chief Lillus?"

"Yes, Sam, it is. What do you have for me on the second female murder victim?"

"I have done DNA testing on the seminal fluids in her vagina and compared it to the DNA taken from the seminal fluids in the other murdered female's vagina and they match!" says Sam.

"So, we know the murderer for each of those girls is the same person," states Julia.

"Yes, it appears so," says Sam.

"Sam, what can you tell me about the butchering of those two females?" asks Julia.

"Julia, the butchering of the female's genitals is very similar. The murder cut them up like cutting meat."

"How so, Sam?"

"The butchering involved slicing the labia off from each of the female's genitals. They both have had their clitoris cut out as well. I also found a gulf ball in each of their vaginas with the inscription 'bitch'."

"Sam, what have you determined to be the cause of death?" asks Julia.

"There are about twenty stab wounds all over their bodies. The stab wound on the inner thigh of each of them is what killed them. The cut was through the Femoral Artery. It does appear that the butchering happened shortly after."

"Thank God, those two didn't have to feel the butchering," says Julia.

"Julia, do you have any leads to who might have murdered these two? They are so young and beautiful. It is such a shame," says Sam.

"No, Sam, but I feel we are getting closer," says Julia.

RICHARD GOES TO THE STRIP CLUB

J ulia asks Richard to visit the strip club.

"Richard, I have a job for you. Do you know the strip joint up on Harrison?" asks Julia.

"Well, I know of it, but I have never been inside," says Richard.

"Of course not. I do want you to go inside tonight and every night throughout the week," says Julia.

"How will I explain this to Bobbie?"

"Take her along if you would like. Some woman like to watch other women..."

"Chief Lillus, are you suggesting...?"

"Not at all, I just know no one inside that place will bat an eye seeing a female in there, who isn't pole dancing, etc."

"What do you want me to do while visiting the place?"

"I want you to blend in and keep an eye out for Mr. Fulmer," says Julia.

"Mr. Fulmer? Why do you think he would be there?" asks Richard.

"Fucking college girls and possibly his daughter; I would suspect he would be there as well."

"Yeah, but those girls pole dancing don't fuck patrons."

"Richard! How do you know that?" asks Julia inquisitively.

"I am just guessing..."

"I feel if Fulmer can't keep his penis in his pants, he would be at the strip club getting off when he doesn't have a female to fuck," says Julia.

"OK, I can do it," says Richard.

"Oh, Richard, I think you better take Bobbie with you, just to keep you in line," Julia says jokingly.

RICHARD TRIES TO SEDUCE BOBBIE

R ichard suddenly gets frisky while visiting the strip club with
Bobbie.

"Bobbie, act like you are aroused looking at those pole dancers," says
Richard.

"What, Richard? It doesn't appear you are 'acting' aroused!"
exclaims Bobbie.

"You just wait until we get home, sweetie, and I will show you who
I am aroused by," says Richard.

"Richard, do not touch me. Don't even come close to me. I know
how swift your hands can be and this is the last place I would want to
have your hand on my crotch," says Bobbie.

"How about later, you sexy vixen? Maybe in the car on the way
home?" asks Richard.

"I do not know what I am going to do with you," says Bobbie.

"Well, how about fucking me for starters?" asks Richard.

"Hey, look, you already got me pregnant. What more do you want?
Don't respond Richard!" exclaims Bobbie.

THE SLUT IN THE STRIP CLUB

M iss Darcie, once again, pleases Fred Fulmer with her wares.

"Hey, there is Mr. Fulmer standing in front of the stage. I can see he has his eyes on that broad pole dancing," says Bobbie.

"Let's watch what transpires," says Richard.

"See, he is waving a fistful of money to her," says Bobbie.

"Watch what happens next," says Richard.

"How do you know what happens next, Richard?" asks Bobbie.

"Oh, you must have fallen asleep on those nights when we were watching the television. All sleazy murder mysteries have a strip club with pole dancers," says Richard.

"She is coming over to him...and what the hell..the slut! Did you see that, Richard?"

"I tried not to look."

"She squatted down in front of Fulmer and parted her knees. That bitch has no crotch in her shorts and as plain as day, I saw her snatch. She is a disgusting whore, that bitch!" exclaims Bobbie.

"OK, Bobbie, let's get out of here. We have what we need. Bobbie, would you pole dance for me?"

"Richard, you don't have enough money to have me pole dance," says Bobbie jokingly.

"That's OK, I don't need money to see your...."

"Richard! Come on, let's get out of here!" exclaims Bobbie.

JULIA HAS A PLAN

After listening to the testimony from Richard and Bobbie's visit to the strip club, Julia starts to formulate a plan.

"Julia, we saw Mr. Fulmer at the strip joint last night and you wouldn't believe what those sluts do for money," says Bobbie.

"Well, I have a hunch," says Julia.

"Did it appear Mr. Fulmer was having a good time?" asks Julia.

"He sure was. I wouldn't be a bit surprised if he got off in one of those sluts," says Bobbie.

"Thanks, Bobbie. I have what I need. By the way, how is that little tike you have in your belly?" asks Julia.

"Oh, she is just fine. Kicks a lot and I am not showing that much, am I?" asks Bobbie.

"I can see the start of a baby bump there, Bobbie," responds Julia.

"Have a great weekend Bobbie, I will see you on Monday," says Julia.

"OK, you too, Julia, I still want to go to the gym Wednesday with you. I am starting the prenatal workout routines," says Bobbie.

"You bet, mom," says Julia.

JULIA PAYS A VISIT TO THE STRIP CLUB

"Ma'am, what drink can I get you?"

"I'll just have a club soda, thank you," says Julia.

"I don't see many woman here that are not dancing on a pole," says the bartender.

"I like to watch. They turn me on," answers Julia.

"OK, I see. One club soda coming up."

"Hey bartender, who is that guy flirting with that dancer over there?" asks Julia.

"Oh, he is a regular and she appears to be his private dancer. He must pay well because she does the 'nooky-nooky' for him and later takes him to her private viewing room."

"What may I ask is the 'nooky-nooky'?"

"Well, ma'am. If a patron pays enough money to Miss Darcie, which is that girl's name, she will squat down and show him her, ahem, pussy and I suspect she will allow penetration."

"Oh, how does she do that?"

"She wears crotchless shorts for her routine."

"I would love to see that," says Julia.

"Stick around, I am sure she will do it for him. She always does."

"Do all the dancers do the 'nooky-nooky', as you say?"

"No, the girls are not to get that intimate, but, Miss Darcie? Well, she is special."

"What happens in the private viewing area?"

"Lap dancing, I guess."

" I just work here. I don't participate, but I can't say that I wouldn't want to," says the bartender.

"Yeah, I get what you mean. It gets me off too."

"By the way ma'am, as beautiful as you are, I am surprised you don't want a man."

"I do like men, but I get my best orgasms watching men get off with women," says Julia.

"Do you think I could get into Miss Darcie's viewing room with that guy, to watch?"

"Oh, I do not know about that. Miss Darcie has a steep price for what she does."

"No problem, I will pay. Here, take this fifty to that gentlemen and tell him I will give him and Miss Darcie, each, another fifty if I can join them in the private viewing and watch." says Julia.

"Yeah, sure, I will try."

"Hey honey, I understand you like to watch?" asks Fred Fulmer.

"Yes, I do. I would like to go to Miss Darcie's viewing room and watch."

"It just so happens that Miss Darcie just might accommodate if you were to pay her."

"Take this fifty and give it to her," says Julia.

"Hey, ma'am, I hope you have fun watching. Maybe you can swing by and describe to me what you see in there," says the bartender.

"Hello, Miss Darcie, is it?"

"Yes."

"Thank you for letting me watch. I promise I won't interfere."

"Maybe after I am through with him, you and I could play around a little," suggests Julia.

"Hey, what about me? I would like to play around with you...did I get your name?" asks Fred Fulmer.

"Unzip those pants buster and let me see your cock," orders Miss Darcie.

———

MISS DARCIE PERFORMS HER TYPICAL ROUTINE ON MR. FULMER. SHE STROKES HIS COCK WITH HER MOUTH LONG ENOUGH TO GET HIM AROUSED. SHE, THEN, PROCEEDS TO LAP DANCE WITH HIM WITH HIS COCK INSIDE HER VAGINA. AFTER A FEW MINUTES, MISS DARCIE PULLS HERSELF UP OFF HIS COCK JUST AS HE EJACULATES INTO THE AIR

———

"What did you think?" asks Miss Darcie.

"I was quite aroused, and I did 'cum' a couple of times. Oh, shit, I dropped my business card I was going to give you, Miss Darcie. I don't have time now, but I would like you to call me when you have some free time. I would love to play around with you a bit," says Julia.

"Likewise, we can get off together."

"Great, here is my card."

JULIA, YOU LIKE TO WATCH?

Julia describes, very sheepishly, her visit to the strip club.

"Julia, you did what?" asks Richard and Bobbie.

"I got a semen sample from Mr. Fulmer. I won't go into details because what I had to do was pretty sick, but I needed to get the semen from him to have Sam match it with the two dead females. I feel there will be a match," says Julia.

"Give us a clue of how you actually got the sample?" asks Bobbie.

"Well, let's put it this way. Mr. Fulmer somehow talked the pole dancer into having sex with him while lap dancing."

"Let me guess, Miss Darcie? That slut!" exclaims Bobbie.

"She wouldn't allow him to 'cum' inside her, so she lifted herself up from his cock just in time for him to ejaculate in the air and onto the floor. I purposely dropped my business card on the floor and while I was down picking it up, I was able to get a sample of his semen on the swab," Julia says.

"So, tell me, why were you in the room with them while they were fucking and why would you give Miss Darcie or Mr. Fulmer your business card?" asks Bobbie.

"Well, you see, I pretended I liked to watch, and I promised Miss Darcie I would be back to have a little pussy to pussy fingering," Julia responds sheepishly.

"Julia, you wouldn't, would you?" asks Richard.

"Come on guys you know me better than that. I am heterosexual, and I would only have sex with a man."

"Stop laughing you guys, I had to come up with something to get the sample."

DNA MATCHING

Sam finished getting the DNA test matching from the lab and tries to make a call to Julia, but she beats him to it and calls him.

"Sam! Julia Lillus, here."

"Yes Julia."

"Have you had the chance to check the DNA of the semen sample I gave to you and the DNA found in the dead female vagina's?"

"Yes, Julia, I have just received the report. So, let me see what the results tell us. Julia, we have a match! The semen sample of Mr. Fulmer and the semen found in the dead women's vaginas is an exact match."

"Sam, we have our murderer. Could I give you a bed sheet belonging to Vicky Lynn, the Fulmer's daughter, and see if there is semen on it and if it is a match? I want to nail him on raping his daughter, too"

"Sure, if you can get it to me by tomorrow, I will be able to get results by the end of the week."

"Ok, Sam, thanks. I will be in touch," says Julia.

SOILED BED SHEETS

J ulia sets out to obtain Vicky Lynn's bed sheets so that Sam can
have tests done that can prove the semen stains match the semen
samples of Fred Fulmer.

"Richard and Bobbie, would you please step into my office?" asks
Julia.

"I need you two to go over to the Fulmer's house and bring Mr.
Fulmer here. Be sure to read him his rights, because we are arresting
him for the murder of those two female college students and the rape
of his daughter, Vicky Lynn," says Julia.

"That poor girl," says Bobbie.

"We still need to find her. I would like her to take the stand in
court in order to convict him of the rape," says Julia.

"Mrs. Fulmer?"

"Yes."

"This is Chief Julia Lillus. Do you still have Vicky Lynn's soiled bed sheet?"

"Yes, I do."

"Would you please bring it down to the Police Station?"

"Why, what did you find?" asks Ethel.

"We have no conclusive evidence yet, but we think your husband has been raping Vicky Lynn. I want you to be very careful around him. I suggest you go visit someone for the next couple of days," says Julia.

"Oh, my God, my poor Vicky Lynn, that bastard..I will kill him!" exclaims Ethel.

"Mrs. Fulmer, please, go visit a relative for the next couple of days. We will handle your husband," says Julia.

THREAT FROM A BUTCHER

Fred Fulmer calls in sick to work and has an agenda for his wife, Ethel.

"Fred, are you supposed to be at work?" asks Ethel.

"I am taking the day off. We are going to get to know each other today and there will be no excuses!" says Fred.

"I told you I am going to see my sister today," says Ethel.

"You aren't going anywhere! You are going to stay here and I am going to fuck you!"

"Fred, I told you, I do not want to have sex with you and I won't!"

"You will or I will make sure you can't have sex ever again!"

"Fred, what the hell is the matter with you?"

"I am a man and I have man feelings; I am going to fuck you, Ethel!"

"Fred, why do you have that knife?"

"I told you, if you don't lie down on that bed."

"Fred, you threatening me with that knife? I am calling the police. You are crazy!"

"I said lie down!"

"Don't push me!"

"Get those panties off and spread those legs!"

"No, Fred! I am not afraid of you!"

"Look, bitch! If you don't allow me between those legs, I am going to start cutting you! Those other bitches wouldn't fuck me, so I fixed them...yeah I fixed them!"

"Fred, what the hell are you talking about? What women and what did you do to Vicky Lynn..."

Suddenly, there is a knock at the door of the Fulmer's house.

"Hello, Mr. and Mrs. Fulmer, this is the Harford Police Department Deputies. Please let us in."

"So, Fred, you better put that knife away unless you want them to see what you are trying to do to me, And, oh, Fred, you can't get your way with me. Now, they are here to take you away!" exclaims Ethel.

"Hell, no, they have no proof..."

THE ARREST

F red Fulmer's crimes catch up with him.

———————————

"Mr. Fred Fulmer, you have the right to remain silent. Anything you say can and will be used against you in the court of law," says Richard.

"Why are you arresting me?" asks Fred.

"You are being arrested for the rape and murder of two college girls," answers Bobbie.

"Thank God you came! He was just about to murder me too!" exclaims Ethel.

"You, bitch! Officers, we were about to…"

"Come on, Mr. Fulmer, get in the car," says Richard.

PROOF VICKY LYNN WAS RAPED

Conclusive evidence has come from the tests on the semen stains, that Fred Fulmer has been raping his daughter Vicky Lynn.

"Julia, Sam is on the line for you," says Betsy.

"Thanks, Betsy, put him through."

"Sam, what do you have?"

"Julia, there are semen stains on the Fulmer's daughter's bed sheet and the DNA results match up with the DNA of Mr. Fulmer's semen samples."

"That bastard is raping his own daughter!" exclaims Julia.

"Talk to you later, Julia."

"Thanks, Sam."

I HAVE RIGHTS

Fred Fulmer pleads to the Harford Police Department he is being detained wrongly.

"Julia, Richard and Bobbie are here," says Betsy.

"Ok, I will be right out," says Julia.

"Mr. Fulmer, please have a seat!"

"You, you...are the one who likes to watch! It was all a setup, wasn't it?" asks Mr. Fulmer.

"Mr. Fulmer, it appears that you have been pussy sniffing around quite a bit," says Julia.

"You got it all wrong! I paid to fuck her!"

"Let me get straight to the facts, Mr. Fulmer. You raped and murdered two college females and you have been raping your daughter! You just can't keep your cock in your pants, can you?" asks Julia.

"Richard, lock him up!"

"You will pay for this, bitch! It was a setup! I have might rights!" exclaims Mr. Fulmer.

"Fulmer! You have no rights! May you burn in hell!" exclaims Julia.

VICKY LYNN IS FOUND

Nicole has made a new friend at the Home for Young Mothers.

"Hello, Julia, how was your day today?" asks Nicole.

"It was the typical day, Nicole. How was your day Nicole?"

"I have been attending the Home for Young Mothers for a couple of months, now, and I finally made a friend."

"Oh, great, what is her name?"

"Her name is Vicky Lynn."

"Where is she from; where is her home?"

"She hasn't said. She is the quiet type."

"How many weeks pregnant is she?"

"She thinks she is eight weeks. The results from the clinic haven't come in yet."

"Does she know who the father is?"

"I don't know. Every time I ask her, she starts to cry."

"Nicole, I think you should invite Vicky Lynn over for dinner sometime?"

"That would be great, Julia. Thank you!"

"Mrs. Fulmer, this is Chief Lillus, I have some good news for you."

"Yes, what is it?"

"I have found Vicky Lynn."

"Oh, where is she? Is she all right?"

"Yes, she is currently staying at the Home for Young Mothers."

"Oh, no! My Vicky is pregnant?"

"She thinks she is at least eight weeks pregnant," says Julia.

"Who is the father," asks Mrs. Fulmer.

"I don't know, she doesn't say."

"Do you think the father is my husband Fred?" asks Mrs. Fulmer.

"We don't know, but it is possible. Tests cannot be done this early in her pregnancy without possibly causing a miscarriage," says Julia.

"Do you think I can go see her?"

"Mrs. Fulmer, I think you should stay away for a while, at least until after the trial," says Julia.

DISTRICT ATTORNEY GOLDSMITH

J ulia has to talk to the district attorney concerning the Fred
Fulmer murder case.

"Thank you, District Attorney Goldsmith, for allowing me to talk to
you about the Fulmer case," says Julia.

"It is my pleasure, Chief Lillus. So, what do we have with this
case?"

"We have conclusive DNA evidence that Mr. Fred Fulmer had sex
with each of the two female college students. From our surveillance,
we found that Mr. Fulmer frequents the college and initiates sex with
female students in the back seat of his car, on campus. The Fulmer's
daughter, Vicky Lynn, became missing until yesterday when I
discovered she is at the Home for Young Mothers; she is eight weeks
pregnant."

"Is the father of her baby Mr. Fulmer?" asks district attorney
Goldsmith.

"It is interesting you mention that because we also have DNA evidence of Mr. Fulmer's semen on Vicky Lynn's bedsheets. It appears that he is the father of her baby," says Julia.

"What hurdles do we have in getting a conviction for the murder of those two women?" asks District Attorney Goldsmith.

"We can prove Mr. Fulmer had sex with those women, but we cannot tie him to the murder of them. It is possible he had sex with them at an earlier time before someone else committed the murders. We can't do anything about his daughter. She is too early in her pregnancy to get a safe paternity test, so we cannot convict him on rape and endangering a minor."

"How old is Mr. Fulmer's daughter?" asks District Attorney Goldsmith.

"She is fourteen years old," answers Julia.

"So, at this time without a murder weapon and a way to tie it to Mr. Fulmer, he walks," says District Attorney Goldsmith.

"We could try to get his daughter on the stand, but without a paternity test, we have no proof he is the father of her baby and without some kind of witness, it would be hard to prove rape, even though I am sure it was," says Julia.

"Well, Chief Lillus, you are going to have to release Mr. Fulmer until you can find concrete proof he murdered those females."

RELEASE HIM

Julia reluctantly gives the order to release Fred Fulmer's detainment.

"Richard, please release Mr. Fulmer," says Julia.

"What? What happened?" asks Richard.

"We don't have enough evidence to prove he murdered those females. The only thing we can prove is that he is getting off on quite a few females around town. I definitely believe all involved have been raped, but we don't have anyone alive to prove it," says Julia.

"We need to find the murder weapon!" says Richard.

"Mr. Fulmer, you are free to go," says Richard.

"Where is that bitch Chief of yours?" asks Fred Fulmer.

"What do you want, Fulmer? You are released," says Julia.

"I told you all of this is bull shit! You don't have anything on me!" exclaims Fred Fulmer.

"Just watch your step. We will be watching you. It is just a matter of time you will slip up and then you will be back in here," says Julia.

"Listen, sweetheart, instead of watching Miss Darcie and I, why don't you sit that sweet ass of yours on my cock! I would love it knowing I fucked a Police Chief!" exclaims Fred Fulmer.

Julia pulls her hand back and swiftly releases, as her hand swipes across Fred Fulmer's face.

"I'll take that as a yes to my invitation, honey. See ya around," says Fred Fulmer as he leaves the department building.

"What is the next step, Julia?" asks Bobbie.

"The first thing we need to make sure is that Mrs. Fulmer does not tell her husband of Vicky Lynn's whereabouts," says Julia.

THE CONFESSION

Ethel Fulmer opens up to Julia to what transpired when Fred found her at their home before she could leave for safety.

"Mrs. Fulmer, this is Chief Julia Lillus. Your husband has been released. You do not have time for me to explain. You need to get out of your house now! I a sure he is headed to your home and he is not to be trusted," says Julia.

"Oh, my, yes, he is a monster!" exclaims Mrs. Fulmer.

"Get out now, Ethel!"

"Where the hell you are going, Ethel?" asks Fred.

"I am going out to do an errand," replies Ethel.

"Oh no you are not! We are going to finish where we left off before we were interrupted by those 'Keystone Cops'!"

"Fred, I told you, I am not interested in having sex with you, now I am going!"

"Get the hell over here, Ethel!"

"You are hurting my arm, Fred!"

"Look, I don't want any shit from you! Those damn bitches gave me all sorts of shit. I am lucky I could 'cum' with those cunts. I fixed them, though. After I forced them at knife point to lay still, I fucked them, and I fucked them hard. Afterward, I had to reward them for their despondence. I stuffed a rag into their mouths and I dressed out their pussies. I trimmed off their pussy lips and then I cut out their clits. You should have seen how neat I was with my butchering. They were in so much pain, I decided to put them out of their misery. I stabbed them a couple of times and then I started to get hard again, so I kept stabbing them."

"Fred, you murdered them? You're a sick bastard! You will never get away with this!"

"How do you figure, Ethel? I might even get a hard-on when I am trimming your pussy, and then, I told you what happens."

"Fred tell me something, did you rape and kill that girl found in our chest freezer?"

"I sure as hell did! Now, that bitch could fuck, or should I say she had a tight pussy. I will bet I was the first one to penetrate her ass. I put her in the freezer because I couldn't figure what to do with her and I didn't want her to start stinking."

"You actually fucked her in our house, Fred?"

"Don't get so excited, Ethel. Do you think I would desecrate our bed with fucking that broad there? No, I used Vicky Lynn's bed. I hope she isn't too upset with her soiled bed sheets."

"Fred, you have gone crazy! Why don't you put that knife down and get some help? We can go together."

"Oh, no, Ethel, I don't need help! I am a typical male and I need to get 'laid' often. If you would be a wife to me and satisfy me, I wouldn't have had to fuck those other bitches."

"Fred, put that knife down!"

"No, Ethel! Get on the bed now!"

"Fred, I will follow all of your orders and fuck you if you just put that knife down. I need to go into the bathroom to get some vaginal lubricant, so I don't get sore. I promise I will be the wife you want."

"OK, Ethel, but this knife will be in arms reach if you pull something!"

"Fred, I will fuck you as you wish."

THE DEADLY TRAP

Ethel walks into the bathroom and, first, takes a pee, then goes into the medicine cabinet for the vaginal lubricant and the applicator. She fills the applicator and inserts it into her vagina pushing the lubricant in.

"OK, Fred, I am ready for you. Would you like me to lie on the bed? Doggy-style or missionary?"

"Ethel, I will call the shots!"

"I will remove my shirt and panties."

"Ethel, stop it! I will tell you when I want your clothes off!"

"Fred, I think you should stop playing with yourself and penetrate me!"

"Shut up, Ethel!"

"Would you like some help, Fred?"

"Ethel, I have had it! Shut up so I can get hard!"

"I am ready, Fred. What is the matter, did you wear yourself out?"

"Ethel, you are not turning me on like those other bitches!"

"Fred, you promised, now put down that knife!"

"You are being despondent, and you don't turn me on, so I am going to carve your pussy!"

"Wait just a minute, Fred. Let me try one more thing that will assure you become hard."

"Ethel, stop telling me what to do! I am in charge! I am always in charge!"

"Fred, I am being a wife and helping you pursue avenues which will get you the pleasure you desire in having sex, now come up here and straddle my head with your knees. I will get you hard quickly. OK, now, place your dick right here in my mouth and I will suck you. Yeah just like that."

"Ah…Oh..ouch! Ethel, you bitch! I am going to cut you up, now!"

"No, you won't Fred, because you won't live that long. You will bleed to death in a matter of minutes. I severed both of your femoral arteries in your thighs. Die, you bastard and burn in hell! Now, get off me!"

HE IS DEAD

E thel must call Chief Lillus and tell her that her husband Fred
Fulmer is no longer a threat to her.

"Hello, this is Ethel Fulmer. I would like to speak with Chief Lillus."

"Just a minute while I see if she is in her office," says Betsy.

"Chief, Mrs. Fulmer is on the other line."

"Thanks, Betsy, put her through."

"Hello, Mrs. Fulmer, this is Chief Lillus. What can I do for you?"

"Fred, my husband, killed those college girls after raping them. He
confessed the entire acts to me when I accepted his invitation to have
sex."

"You didn't leave, Ethel?"

"I tried, but he met me at the door and forced me to stay," says
Ethel.

"Ethel, he is dangerous! Are you able to leave now?" asks Julia.

"No need too, Chief, Fred won't hurt anyone anymore."

"Why Ethel? How do you know that?"

"Because, he is dead. I killed him! You better come over here and I will explain everything to you. You can take me in, too," says Ethel.

WHO WAS FRED FULMER?

E thel lays out to Julia what kind of man her husband was and the
monster he became.

"So, Ethel, it sounds like Fred had to be in charge of all his actions and
when he received any type of despondence, he got mad to the point of
a butchering rage and his release was to cut the genitals of the
despondent individuals."

"Yes, exactly."

"He raped and then murdered the victims, stashing one of them in
your chest freezer because he didn't know what to do with the body."

"Yes, that is what he told me."

"You figured out how he was 'ticking' and played into it, at a great
risk, I must say, and sliced his thighs with a razor blade you got from
the bathroom?" asks Julia.

"Yes, that is correct, except he had the knife in his hand and started
to cut me," says Ethel.

"It sounds like self-defense to me," says Julia.

"Look, here are the cuts Fred made on my genitals," explains Ethel as she lifts her skirt and pulls her panties down to expose the lacerations around her vagina.

"You should get to the doctors and have those lacerations properly taken care of to ward off infection. Did he penetrate?" asks Julia.

"No, he couldn't get it up to penetrate. I kept pushing him into decisions he wanted to make, so he couldn't get aroused," says Ethel.

"Now, what about Vicky Lynn? Did he say anything to you about her?" asks Julia.

"No, but he told me that he fucked one of those females in Vicky's bed and was proud he left his semen on her bed sheets," says Ethel.

"I will get the Coroner down her to collect the body. You are free to go, Ethel," says Julia.

"Do you think I can go and see Vicky Lynn, now?" asks Ethel.

"Sure, but take it easy on her. If you two want to talk, my door is always open," says Julia.

"Thank you, Chief Lillus."

"Ethel, you can call me Julia."

VICKY LYNN EXPLAINS

Several weeks have passed since the case of Fred Fulmer was closed. Julia and Nicole are having a quiet dinner in Julia's apartment. There is a knock at the door.

"Well, Hello, Ethel and Vicky Lynn," says Julia.

"Hey, Vicky, how are you? I am so happy to see you," says Nicole.

"Can we talk to you Chief, I mean Julia?" asks Ethel.

"Well, certainly," says Julia.

"Please have a seat Vicky," says Nicole.

"Go ahead, Vicky, you can talk to Julia. She is our friend," says Ethel.

"Mrs. Lillus, I want you to know that I had been forced into having sex by my father for the past two years. I tried to stop him every time, but he scared me into complying. After a while, I felt that maybe he was doing it to me because he loved me, and he told me time after time I was special and by 'doing me' proved it. I was always sore down there because he would 'do it to me' almost every day of the week. Sometimes it was when momma was asleep or out on an errand. I

149

tried to go with her on the errands, but he wouldn't allow it and threatened me if I did. I told him when I started to get my period, I could become pregnant, but that did not stop him."

"Vicky is your father the father of your baby?" asks Julia.

"Yes, he is. I have never had that done to me by anyone else. I wanted to stay a virgin and now I am just a whore!"

"No, Vicky, you are a victim of nonconsensual sex commonly called rape. Your father raped you," says Julia.

"Mrs. Lillus, I do not know what to do about my baby," says Vicky Lynn.

"What do you want for your baby?" asks Julia.

"I don't know. If it were my husband, then I would surely be happy about my baby, but I do not know if I can be happy with this baby under the circumstances," says Vicky Lynn.

"There is counseling services offered free of charge at the Home for Young Mothers geared just for situations such as yours. They will help you make the right decisions," says Julia.

"Vicky, honey, will you be returning to our home?" asks Ethel.

"Momma, I like it at the Home and feel I need some time away from our home for a while. I will always welcome you with open arms when you come visit, momma," says Vicky Lynn.

"Vicky, you are always welcome, here, anytime you want to visit me or Nicole," says Julia.

IT WAS FOR THE BETTER

The aftermath of the entire murder and rape cases has exhausted Julia, Richard, and Bobbie.

"Richard and Bobbie, the Fulmer case was living hell. I thank you two for being very instrumental in solving every facet of it," says Julia.

"I am waiting for the day when we have parking tickets to process or hookers to get off the streets. We all need a vacation!" exclaims Bobbie.

"Chief, Ethel Fulmer is on the other line," says Betsy.

"Thank you, Betsy, put her through."

"Hello, Ethel. How is Vicky Lynn?"

"Vicky is why I am calling, Julia."

"What about Vicky? How is her baby?" asks Julia.

"Julia, Vicky lost her baby last night. She had a miscarriage," says Ethel.

"I am so sorry, Ethel. Is there anything I can do for you or Vicky?" asks Julia.

"Vicky and I feel, under the circumstances, it is for the better. She is home with me now and she is staying. We must both rebuild our lives. We have enrolled into counseling services tailored to our needs," says Ethel.

"Great, Ethel! Vicky Lynn will need quite a bit of those services. Please be sure to keep her motivated to attend her counseling," says Julia.

JULIA IS A MOTHER TO NICOLE

J ulia directs her attention to Nicole and is happy to have her in
her home.

"Nicole, your baby bump is so cute!" exclaims Julia.

"Yeah, great! Easy for you to say. You are not walking like a duck
and have this oversize bowling ball to lug around which is kicking me
all of the time," says Nicole.

"Have you decided who your birthing buddy will be?" asks Julia.

"That is an easy one. It is you, Julia!" exclaims Nicole.

"Well, in that case, let's get going and start attending the birthing
classes," says Julia.

"Julia, do you think my baby will be like Ron? I mean have his
rotten personality and sinister appetite for sex?" asks Nicole.

"Nicole, your baby will be just fine. You are a great mom and the
love you have for your baby won't allow such things," says Julia.

"Julia, you are like a mom to me," says Nicole.

"Nicole, I want to be a mom for you. Let's go to the mall. I need to
get you some new clothes to fit that baby bump," says Julia.

EPILOGUE

J ulia, Richard, and Bobbie continue with the hard work of keeping peace in the city of Harford.

Bobbie and Richard enjoy the birth of a baby girl. Bobbie feels that she has more of Richard's personality and fears that, in the future, she too, will have a hyper sex drive. A smile comes across her face as she reasons it could be a blessing because she wouldn't want Richard any other way. After all, she too, has a hyper sex drive.

"Richard, the baby is asleep. Would you please come into the bedroom with me? Oh, and shut the door....!"

Nicole delivered a beautiful baby girl whose features are a close match to hers. She feels her baby girl doesn't share any of her father's personality. If fact, Nicole does not think about Ron.

Julia has invited Nicole and her baby to stay with her as long as she would like. Nicole is happy staying with her 'mom' and isn't thinking of leaving anytime soon.

Ethel Fulmer and her daughter, Vicky Lynn, continues to attend counseling. Ethel has a renewed relationship with Vicky, while Vicky is studying to become an attorney; specifically a strength in assault prosecutions.

Julia, now and then, thinks back on her own assault initiated by Ron Linden. She is happy that he is no longer around and not in the least concerned where he is or whether he might have been murdered, and if so, by whom.

She is happy with her new appointment to Chief of Police for the Harford Police Department and continues to foster her friendship with Richard and Bobbie in and outside of the office.

Julia feels a motherly connection to Nicole and her new baby. She is happy that Nicole has decided to stay with her. Nicole says Julia is grandma to her baby, while Bobbie says that she is aunt Julia to her new baby.

Even though the love that Julia had in her relationship with Tim is lost, she is replacing it with a different kind of love for those girls and their babies.

ABOUT THE AUTHOR

James Roberts is an emerging author of Murder, Erotic Sex, Rape, and Deceit.

The reader is challenged by the experiences seen through the eyes of his characters, and although fiction in nature, allows the reader to experience real-life situations relatable to their world, and invites the reader to explore their inner feelings of right and wrong based on those experiences.

This is Book Two of A Julia Lillus Series of adult books written by James Roberts.

www.ingramcontent.com/pod-product-compliance
Lightning Source LLC
Chambersburg PA
CBHW052136170626
46812CB00004B/1454